STOUT HEARTS
&
WHIZZING
BISCUITS

A PATRIA STORY
BY

DANIEL McINERNY

ILLUSTRATIONS BY
THEODORE SCHLUENDERFRITZ

Text copyright © 2011 by Daniel McInerny
Published by Trojan Tub Entertainment
ISBN: 0615706673
ISBN-13: 978-0615706672

THIS BOOK IS FOR MISS AMY,
WHO SHOWED ME THE WAY TO PATRIA.

CONTENTS

CHAPTER ONE

THE FIRST BISCUIT IS FIRED

Every once in a great while—perhaps no more than once—life hits you over the head with an adventure. And when it comes to the head of Oliver Stoop, the missile in question was a biscuit. Not one of those moist, yummy, butter-absorbent numbers that your grandmother pulls out of the oven on Sunday mornings. No, in Oliver Stoop's case we're talking about a biscuit with which something had gone horribly wrong. Was it too much shortening? The wrong kind of flour? Maybe it was simply overcooked? It is difficult to say. What is clear, is that the biscuit that plunked Oliver Stoop on the head was as hard as a hockey puck.

And after it hit him, Oliver Stoop's life was never the same again.

Oliver's strange encounter with this biscuit occurred one bright June morning soon after his family had moved to a remote piece of land in the country. The Stoops—Mr. and Mrs. Stoop, Oliver, and Mrs. Stoop's sister, Hazel — were living on their new property in a mobile home until construction was completed on their new house — what Mr. Stoop liked to call his "dream castle." On this morning, Oliver was seated at the kitchen table demolishing his second bowl of Captain Cocoa's Fabulous Fudge Rockets (with 8 Essential Vitamins Plus Iron!). He was reading a story from his favorite series of books, *The Chronicles of Odysseus Murgatroyd, Adventurer, as Narrated by His Faithful Potawatomi Scout, Turkey Beard*. He was just slurping up the last of the fudge-flavored milk when his father came in from outside.

"Good morning, Oliver," said Mr. Stoop sternly.

"Good morning," mumbled Oliver. His heart was thumping. He knew what his father wanted to talk to him about.

"Any bogey men attack you from out of the woods last night?"

Oliver stared into his empty cereal bowl and shook his head.

"I didn't think so," frowned Mr. Stoop. "Now son, I want you to promise that you will never, and I mean never, call the police emergency number again *unless it's a real emergency*."

"But Dad!" cried Oliver. "I saw *people* moving out there along the edge of the woods. I *really* did."

"The police weren't very happy with you, Oliver. It took them over an hour just to find this place, and I didn't have a donut to offer them. Now I want you to *promise me,* you will *never* do that again."

Mr. Stoop waited for Oliver's reply. What was he to do? Renounce all police aid and comfort when there were marauders on the prowl? Or should he lie, to his father no less, by making a false promise?

It reminded Oliver of one of the stories from the *Chronicles of Odysseus Murgatroyd,* a story called "Irritations Among the Iroquois." Oliver was thinking of that point in the story when Odysseus Murgatroyd and Turkey Beard were escaping downriver in their canoe, only to realize that in hot pursuit of them was a canoe full of nasty Iroquois warriors unhappy with Turkey Beard for proposing marriage to their sister. While the Iroquois canoe was still some distance away, Odysseus Murgatroyd ordered Turkey Beard to hide himself under a pile of beaver pelts:

And when the Iroquois canoe came even with ours, one of the Iroquois warriors addressed Odysseus:

"Have you seen a Potawatomi scout who thinks him good enough to marry Iroquois princess?"

The warrior didn't really expect the white man to understand him, yet Odysseus replied in flawless

Iroquois:

"He's quite nearby. I last saw him in a canoe."

The Iroquois' eyebrows jerked upward.

"Thanks much, honorable white man."

And he and his band, assuming—falsely—that Odysseus meant that he had seen me pass him in my own canoe, paddled on.

"Fast thinking," I said to Odysseus, lifting a pelt from my face and smiling with admiration at my old friend.

"It is beneath me to lie, Turkey Beard, even to a band of Iroquois warriors seeking a scalp," said Odysseus complacently. "It is perfectly true that you are quite nearby, and that I last saw you in a canoe."

Now Oliver, frightened as he was, in no way wanted to fall short of the high moral standards of Odysseus Murgatroyd. So, weighing his words carefully, he said:

"I promise I won't call the police again *unless it's absolutely necessary.*"

Of course, to Oliver's way of thinking, when could it be more necessary to call the police than when a band of bloodthirsty highwaymen is seeking to attack one's family?

"Excellent, Oliver," smiled Mr. Stoop. "Now get yourself changed and come outside. I have something to show you."

Oliver's bedroom was a tent pitched in the middle of the tiny family room. His Aunt Hazel, who had come to live them a few months before, had taken over what might have been his bedroom.

Oliver crawled back inside his tent and changed out of his threadbare, medieval knight pajamas and into a t-shirt and a pair of jeans that didn't even come close to reaching his ankles. Oliver was tall for his age, and slim, with a head of brown hair that perpetually looked like it had been hanging out the window of a car going ninety miles per hour.

Outside, he found his father standing next to a lawn mower parked under a tree by the new utility shed.

Correction.

To call the Lawn Beast X-Pro Groundskeeper 6000 a *lawn mower* is like calling a Porsche racing car a horseless carriage. A black metallic beauty with scarlet piping, golden hubcaps, and a Corinthian leather captain's chair, the Lawn Beast boasted a turbocharged, two-stroke diesel engine, a 5-speed manual shift, and hi-lo halogen headlights. Oliver's father had also opted for the full gamut of accessories, including a sun-protection canopy, DVD player, and multiple beverage holder.

The Lawn Beast was a sight to behold, and Mr. Stoop was very proud of her. So proud, that you could have knocked Oliver down with a feather when Mr. Stoop declared that for the Lawn Beast's maiden voyage he wanted Oliver to be the captain.

"You want *me* to ride it?"

"Oliver," Mr. Stoop explained as he lifted his son onto the Lawn Beast, "you're getting to be a big boy. How old are you now? Twelve?"

"Eleven."

"Eleven. Exactly my point. You're old enough now to take on adult responsibilities, to put in a man's day full of honest toil and sweat, to go to bed with your muscles aching and in full knowledge that you've really *done* something."

Oliver began to get really worried.

"And this is just the place to do it," said Mr. Stoop, sucking in his breath and glancing at the field and woods with the fresh pride of ownership. "Country living, Oliver. There's nothing like it."

All Oliver could think about were the firemen pulling him out of the twisted wreckage of the mower when he plowed it into the mobile home.

Mr. Stoop showed Oliver the basic operations of the Lawn Beast, and left him to cut the wild grass in the field while he drove into Portage Head for more gas.

"Don't take her out of first gear, son. You can't imagine the awesome power of the Lawn Beast in the higher gears!"

The Lawn Beast in first gear turned out to be a mere kitten, and Oliver soon realized there was nothing to be afraid of. In fact, it wasn't long before he got bored puttering back and forth through the field. It was then he had a brilliant idea. He put the Lawn Beast in neutral and ran inside to get one of the *Chronicles* out of his tent. Puttering through the field on the Lawn Beast was much more enjoyable with the *Chronicles* spread open across the steering wheel.

Oliver, in fact, became so engrossed in the story that he didn't notice himself cutting a wobbly line farther and farther from the house towards the woods. Only when the biscuit plunked him in the head was Oliver's attention diverted.

"OW!" he wailed, turning off the Lawn Beast and rubbing his head.

He looked all about him on the ground, expecting to find a stone. Instead, he found a biscuit.

Someone had just hit him in the head *with a biscuit*—and not a fresh one at that.

While Oliver was examining the odd missile, something clanked against the side of the Lawn Beast's shining frame. It was an *arrow*!

Then a boy sprang from the woods. Barefoot, and as quick as a rabbit, he raced across the field toward Oliver as his long dark hair, tied in a ponytail, bounced joyfully behind him. He looked like some kind of Indian boy, with his brown skin and buckskin pants with no shirt.

He was joined by several more kid Indians, bowstrings taught and arrows twitching.

Oliver wondered. Were these kids the ones he had seen prowling along the edge of the woods the night before?

He lifted his arms in surrender.

"Me no enemy," he said. "Me want peace. Name: O-li-ver. You like chocolate cereal? Me have heap big plenty inside. Give you if me go free."

One of the kid Indians stepped forward:

"Actually, it's *I* am not your enemy. *I* want to go free. Don't you study grammar?"

Oliver gaped at the kid.

"You speak English?"

"Better than you do, I should say."

Oliver inquired politely: "Excuse me, but is this a game?"

The question was answered by another boy coming out of the woods: "Yeah, it's called "Kick the Uslurper Off Your Land.""

This new boy was no kid Indian. He was as pale-faced as Oliver, but dressed how Oliver imagined a medieval squire would dress, that is, in a long tunic, leather pants, and boots. He carried a strange weapon, what looked to Oliver like a kind of homemade air gun. He walked over to Oliver and picked up the biscuit off the grass and returned it to a bag slung over his shoulder.

"We're at war, my ambuscaded friend. On your knees."

"I'm all for a good game of war," Oliver did his best to smile as he dismounted the Lawn Beast and sunk down on his knees. "What side can I be on?"

"How about the side that gets scalped?" returned the pale-faced boy.

Oliver giggled nervously. When these kids got into a game, they really got into a game. Oliver, at any rate, was dearly hoping it was a game. The fun became even more real when the kid Indian he had been negotiating with whipped a bear knife out of his buckskin sheath. He came over to Oliver and grabbed a chunk of his hair by the pale roots.

"Whoa!" Oliver begged playfully. "Please don't kill me! I have a wife and eight young'uns back in the cabin."

The kid Indian with the bear knife looked wearily at the boy with the strange air gun.

"Get on with it, Flying Squirrel," barked the boy.

Oliver let out an only half pretend yelp as Flying Squirrel pressed the cold steel of the bear knife against the back of his bared neck.

Oliver closed his eyes for effect, preparing to wail in terror when Flying Squirrel began "scalping" him. But nothing happened. The cold steel of the bear knife was removed. His chunk of hair was released. Oliver opened his eyes to find every one of the kid Indians standing at attention, head bowed. More fantastic still, a girl had appeared in the field bestride a magnificent white horse.

CHAPTER TWO

WAR CLOUDS GATHER

W "hat is this place?" the girl asked breathlessly as she guided her steed into the field. "Is this a *fairy land*?"

The figure of Oliver, still on his knees, finally caught her attention.

"And who is this? Is this a little elfin boy? Hello, little elfin boy! My name is Princess Rose, Princess Rose of Patria. Can you understand me, little elfin boy, or do you speak some strange, elfin language?"

The girl—whose every article of clothing, from her dress to her boots to her gloves to her horse's saddle, was the color of *rose*—slid from her horse and rushed over to Oliver as the kid Indians fell out of her way like bowling pins. For all the girl's rosiness, the boys seemed to be deathly afraid of her.

"Do not be afraid, little elfin boy! I am your friend. Tell me, what is this place? What do you call this land? How did I enter it—is there an invisible doorway among the trees, or did you put a spell on me?"

Oliver was not entirely sure how to respond.

"Oh, forgive me!" the girl cried, slapping two rose-gloved hands against her rosy cheeks. "You do not speak our language."

"No," Oliver stammered. "I mean yes. I *do* speak English."

"Good heavens!" the girl squealed delightedly. "The little elfin boy speaks our language!"

Several of the kid Indians had to muffle their snickering laughter.

"Actually," Oliver said, "I'm not a little elfin boy."

"You're *not*?" The girl was clearly disappointed. "What are you? What is your name?"

"I'm Oliver. Oliver Stoop. I live right over there—"

The girl stared curiously across the field. At the same moment one of the kid Indians who had hopped up on the Lawn Beast figured out how to turn it on. Several other kid Indians leapt aboard, and they began to zoom around the field like cats upon a bucking bronco.

"Is that where you live?" the girl asked, looking with some confusion at the mobile home.

"No. Yes. I mean, we're just living there temporarily. My father is still working with the architect on the design of his "dream castle." That's what he calls it."

"Your father is a knight?"

"Knight?" said Oliver. "He's President of the Republic of Staplers."

"The Republic of Staplers! Is that the name of this land?"

"Well—"

But before Oliver could clarify that his father worked for a company that *made* staplers, the girl said:

"Master Oliver, come show me your magical land!"

"Hey!" shouted the pale-faced boy. "He's our prisoner!"

"*Shut it, Farnsworth,*" snapped the girl, the serpent's sting of her voice making it unmistakably clear that she was Farnsworth's older sister. She then turned on Flying Squirrel:

"Put that knife away, squirrel brain!"

Flying Squirrel hesitated—which turned out to be a big mistake. The girl grabbed his ear and twisted until Flying Squirrel's knees buckled and he fell writhing upon the ground. The girl then grabbed Oliver's hand and dragged him after her as she went racing across the field.

For the record, it should be stated that Oliver was not in the habit of holding hands with girls. And even if he were, it is doubtful he would have extended the privilege to a strange girl who called herself a "princess" and who had just appeared out of the woods riding a white horse. Nonetheless, here he was being hauled across the field, his sweaty paw in the grasp of the girl's rose-gloved hand.

"It's the Republic of Staplers!" she sang as she began to twirl Oliver.

"There's no need to twirl," Oliver winced, suddenly very glad that his father was in town and his mother and Aunt Hazel had gone outlet shopping. "Please stop twirling. There's no twirling in the Republic of Staplers!"

"But it's so *exciting*!" the girl cried, breathless and dizzy as she let Oliver go. "Tell me, Master Oliver, about the other magical elements of your land. Are there any fairies here? Gnomes? *Witches*? Tell me there are witches!"

"There's my aunt," Oliver said.

"What's her name?"

"Hazel."

"Witch Hazel! How thrilling! I *love* the Republic of Staplers!"

The Lawn Beast sped past Oliver. She romped across the field while three kid Indians fought one another for control of the steering wheel, and three others hammered away at the chassis with their hatchets.

"What is that strange mechanical contraption?"

queried the girl.

"I don't know who you all are," said Oliver, his dander not only up, but dressed and ready for action. "But I don't really appreciate your game. That's my dad's brand new lawn mower."

The girl looked hurt.

"I told you who I am, Master Oliver. I am Princess Rose of Patria. I'm sorry if we did anything to upset you."

In a voice suddenly transformed into that of a football coach unhappy with his team's performance, the girl roared: "*Get down from that contraption, you morons!*"

The kid Indians managed to still the Lawn Beast and join the rest of their comrades circling around the girl and Oliver.

"Patria aims to live in peace with all the fair folk of the Republic of Staplers," declared the girl haughtily.

"We'll have no talk of peace!" shouted Farnsworth. "This man is a uslurper and deserves to be scalped!"

The kid Indians erupted in a chorus of war-whoops.

"It's *usurper*, bug brain," sneered the girl.

"I have no idea what it means anyway," said Farnsworth.

"It means invader," explained the girl.

"That's right," Farnsworth faced Oliver. "You're a uslurping invader. The Cow Park belongs to Patria."

"What's the Cow Park?" asked Oliver.

"This field," shot back Farnsworth, looking around. "It's Patrian land. It's been called the Cow Park since the time of the dinosaurs!"

Oliver considered this. "That doesn't make any sense," he said.

"What do I care about making sense? This is *war*. Patria is ready to fight to the death!"

"What's a poor princess to do, Master Oliver?" said the girl. "I'm caught between my duty to my country and my magical new friends in the Republic of Staplers! I suppose I must serve my country first. Master Oliver, on behalf of my grandfather, Evander Jolly IV, King of Patria, please tell your father that he must surrender the Cow Park, or else prepare to meet the avenging sword of Patria in battle. *Get me Hecuba, dimwit!*"

This last command had been fired in the direction of an idle kid Indian. As the frightened minion led over her white steed, Oliver wondered at this strange girl. She reminded him of a girl he knew at school, Ramona Cathcart, who, when she wasn't using her black belt in karate to beat up boys in the playground, spent her time filling notebooks with drawings of her own made-up fantasy land called Splortch.

With the kid Indian's assistance the girl remounted her steed.

"Do not despair, Master Oliver," she announced from the great animal's height. "Even though duty keeps me on one side of the battle line, I will forever work to protect the rights of the goodly folk of Staplers. I will help you find a new home. Adieu, my troubled young friend! Adieu!"

"Adieu yourself," Oliver muttered as the girl galloped away across the field and into the woods, a silken scarf of rose billowing behind her. Farnsworth and the band of kid Indians taunted Oliver with menacing stares before following after the girl.

When they had all disappeared into the woods, Oliver went over and examined the scarred Lawn Beast.

"What a bunch of kooks!" he said aloud, then quickly looked over his shoulder to make sure that no one had heard him.

CHAPTER THREE
THE MYSTERIOUS MR. BLAGGARD & MR. SQUILCH

Mr. Stoop came home from the gas station not a little shocked to find his brand new Lawn Beast looking like she had been mugged by a jealous push mower. Her sun canopy was slumped over her steering wheel, her DVD screen cracked, and her body as nicked as a carving board.

"Answer me, Oliver," Mr. Stoop whimpered as he surveyed the damage. *What happened?*

Oliver took a deep breath and let the truth rip.

"These kid Indians came out of the woods, Dad, along with this boy and girl who said they were a prince and princess from a land called Patria—"

That was as far as Oliver got before his father sent him to his tent.

Wiling away the rest of the day in his tent, Oliver couldn't stop thinking about the weird encounter out in the field. Were those boys really Indians? Was that kid Farnsworth really a prince, and his sister a princess? Where did they all go when they retreated into the woods?

"Tell your father, Master Oliver, that he must surrender the Cow Park, or else prepare to meet the avenging sword of Patria in battle!"

While Oliver serves his sentence in his tent, we might make good use of the time by considering just how the family Stoop came to live in a mobile home in this remote corner of northern Indiana.

It all began with Mr. Stoop's promotion at work.

Mr. Stoop had been Vice-President for Coiled Springs at the Republic of Staplers for over ten years, until one day his loyalty, not to mention his cleverness at unjamming jammed staplers, had been rewarded. He was promoted to the office of president—the big cheese, the head honcho, the staple that holds all the pages together.

Along with the promotion came a nifty raise in salary—"a very pretty raise" he said to Mrs. Stoop the night he came home with champagne and brownies and broke the news to the family. That same night, he announced what he planned to do with all this new money: he was finally going to build his dream house—his "castle"—out in the country.

"We're going to get ourselves away from all these noisy neighbors," he proclaimed to Mrs.

Stoop. "I want to be out in the middle of nowhere. I don't want to even *see* another house anywhere on my horizon."

Mr. Stoop hired an architect to draw up the plans based upon the sketches that for years he had been doodling on phone pads and paper napkins. The house would have real turrets, a drawbridge for a garage door, and, yes, a "moat" (in fact, a stream) that would pass under a driveway that rose into a little bridge. There would be an indoor swimming pool and, built onto its roof, a patio with a large awning under which Mr. Stoop could drink his beer and survey his land in peace.

As for this land, Mr. Stoop insisted upon a large open field. This was because Mr. Stoop was a proud member of the Midwest War-Historical Re-Enactment Association. You've probably seen such characters, dressed up in replica military uniforms, acting out famous battles from history. Mr. Stoop and his "team" were specialists in a wide variety of Revolutionary, French & Indian, and Civil War scenarios, and in the summers traveled the Midwest putting on shows at various parks and county fairs. The "battlefield" next to Stoop Castle would give them the ideal place in which to practice.

But finding the right land proved to be a problem. At first Mr. Stoop hired a real estate agent named Wendi. She wore bright purple eye shadow, chewed lots of gum, and had big hair full of colors and glinting highlights that reminded Oliver of a Caramel Super Swirl Sundae from Mister Moo's. Wendi took Mr. and Mrs. Stoop to see various parcels of land out in the more rural parts of the county, but none of them fired Mr. Stoop's imagination. They were either flat, boring farmland or within sight of a neighbor. In the end, Mr. Stoop fired Wendi and announced that to get the job done right he would have to do it himself.

He began by taking an ad out in the newspaper, which appeared both in the print version of the paper and on the Internet:

WANTED
Extremely large, extremely secluded non-farming rural property for construction of family's dream castle by new president of extremely important company. Extreme seclusion an absolute must. Neighbors extremely undesirable. Big open field an extreme necessity. Call nights: 232-2960 or send email to stoop@republicofstaplers.com.

Nothing happened. There were no calls. No emails. So every night after work and all day Saturday and Sunday Mr. Stoop would take his map and drive the back roads within a fifty-mile radius of Portage Head, looking for just the right parcel of land for sale. But he could never find anything that was just right. Mrs. Stoop took to picking up flyers advertising big new houses in town, some with their own indoor swimming pools, small lakes, and paddocks for horses. Yet Mr. Stoop would toss them aside as if Mrs. Stoop were proposing they live in a cardboard box.

"This house has three acres!" Mrs. Stoop cried. "You'd need a telescope even to *find* the neighbors."

"It has no turrets," grumbled Mr. Stoop. "There's no drawbridge!"

"Do we *need* a drawbridge?"

"For twenty years I've gotten up at five-thirty in the morning to go to work, and from now on, when I get home tired in the evenings, I want to drive my car over a moat and through a drawbridge into the garage. Is that too much to ask? I mean, is it?"

It seemed to be. For several more weeks there were no responses to Mr. Stoop's ad.

Until one warm, breezy evening in May there came a knock at the door. Oliver put aside his book and ran to get it. When he swung open the door he stepped back in surprise. Before him were two men wearing the most ridiculous tuxedos he had ever seen. The tuxedo of the man in front was lime green, while the tuxedo of the man behind him was the color of orange sherbet. Each wore a top hat that matched the color of his tuxedo, along with white leather shoes and sunglasses.

"How d'ye do, my young master?" smiled the man in front as he touched the brim of his hat and peeled away his sunglasses. "Permit me to introduce myself. My name is Mr. Blaggard. This is my associate, Mr. Squilch."

This Mr. Blaggard, though rather ugly with his beaky nose, bulging eyes, and pointy chin beard, was an Adonis compared to his partner. Mr. Squilch's hair, which fell all the way to his shoulders, was stringy and unkempt; his unshaven face was dirty with what looked like leftovers from his past three meals; and he had several teeth missing. To Oliver he looked like a rotten jack-o'-lantern, the soggy kind that you see on some porches a week after Halloween.

"I'm wondering," inquired Mr. Blaggard, "if your paternal parent is at home?"

"Huh?" said Oliver.

"Your *father*, boy. May we talk to him?"

Oliver asked them to wait while he went to get his father. When Mr. Stoop appeared at the door, both men greeted him with a resounding: "Yo, dog!"

"I beg your pardon?" grimaced Mr. Stoop as he looked over their absurd tuxedos. "What do you want?"

"We'd like to speak with you about a business proposition," replied Mr. Blaggard.

"No thank you," said Mr. Stoop, and closed the door on them without another word.

"If anyone ever comes again to the house dressed like that," Mr. Stoop warned Oliver, "don't even open the door."

As noted earlier, it was a warm, breezy evening, and the windows along the front of the Stoop home were open to the screens.

"I believe I have the perfect piece of property for you," called out Mr. Blaggard, his beaky nose flattened against the window screen at the bottom of the main stairs.

In a trice Mr. Blaggard and Mr. Squilch were in the kitchen standing before a bewildered Mrs. Stoop and Aunt Hazel.

"Yo, dogs!" Mr. Squilch greeted the ladies as he raised his hand for a high five.

"Why don't we sit here, gentlemen," sang Mr. Stoop, suddenly the soul of hospitality as he offered the two men a seat at the kitchen table.

Mr. Blaggard and Mr. Squilch, it turned out, represented a very wealthy businessman from Antarctica who owned exactly the kind of property that Mr. Stoop was looking for. Five acres. Extremely secluded. Big open field.

So the next morning Oliver and his parents met Mr. Blaggard and Mr. Squilch and toured the property. It wasn't easy getting to it. They had to drive many miles down County Road 6, until they came to the place where Mr. Blaggard and Mr. Squilch had told Mr. Stoop they would be waiting for him. They found them simply standing along the edge of the road, now wearing Bermuda shorts and Hawaiian shirts.

"The entrance is *extremely* private," explained Mr. Blaggard. "You'll have to leave your automobile here."

Mr. Stoop parked the car along the side of the road, and Mr. and Mrs. Stoop and Oliver followed Mr. Blaggard and Mr. Squilch into the woods. Aunt Hazel had no interest in coming. She had told Mr. Stoop that Mr. Blaggard and Mr. Squilch were taking him for a ride. But Mr. Stoop didn't give a fig for his sister-in-law's opinion. He knew what he was doing.

"I'll have you remember, young lady," he crowed, "that I'm the president of a large and extremely powerful company. No one has better business instincts than Reginald Stoop!"

Mr. Blaggard showed them to a footpath in the woods, but it was still another quarter mile or more before they emerged onto a wide, flat piece of land. Most of it was wild grass and weeds, with a few gnarled and ancient trees scattered here and there, and the entirety of it was surrounded by a thick wall of woods. It didn't seem that there was another human being for miles.

As soon as he saw the property, Mr. Stoop knew that his instincts had not let him down. It truly was everything he was looking for.

"How much does your client want for it?" he asked Mr. Blaggard warily.

From the pocket of his Hawaiian shirt Mr. Blaggard took out an envelope and handed it, with an embarrassed smile, to Mr. Stoop. Mr. Stoop opened the envelope and inside found a piece of paper on which was written a price. The price was far, far less than Mr. Stoop ever dreamed he would have to pay.

Mr. Stoop agreed to the price and handed Mr. Blaggard a check for the entire amount then and there. Mr. Blaggard, in turn, handed Mr. Stoop the deed for the property and then everyone shook hands.

After Blaggard and Squilch departed, Mr. Stoop stood with his wife and son and admired his new property.

"Just what I've been dreaming of," he smiled, sucking in his breath. "My own little slice of the American dream, and not a soul even realizes that we're here."

But Mr. Stoop had no idea that, some two hundred miles directly above his balding head, the camera of an unmanned satellite circling the Earth was busily taking photographs of them all at the rate of three per second.

CHAPTER FOUR
KNIGHT EMBASSY

D inner that night was eaten in mournful silence, as though a close family member had died. The only conversation that occurred during the meal was when Mrs. Stoop asked her husband to pass her another microwaveable enchilada, to which Mr. Stoop replied, with a sob stuck in his throat:

"My poor Lawn Beast!"

Oliver gorged his enchilada and excused himself as quickly as he could.

Later that evening, he was reading the *Chronicles* in his tent while his parents watched TV in the family room when there was a loud knock at the front door. Unable to imagine who it could be, Oliver crept out of his tent.

He saw his father standing in the doorway listening to a man who was saying—

"In the name of His Royal Highness, Evander Jolly IV, King of Patria, we are an embassy commissioned to commence parley with you,

President Stoop of the Republic of Staplers, concerning your recent invasion of the territory belonging to the Kingdom of Patria, territory hereafter in these discussions to be referred to as the "Cow Park." We shall enter now and commence parley—"

The man who had uttered these words clanked past Mr. Stoop into the mobile home's tiny family room, and Oliver saw that he was dressed in a full suit of armor. There was more clanking, and then another man in full armor entered the mobile home. As they took their helmets off, Oliver could see that the first was a very old man, while the second was quite younger. There was a sword in each of their scabbards, and on the blue capes they wore draped over one shoulder was a bizarre insignia: a silver shield in the middle of which was a blue sock.

Even more bizarre, the two armored knights were followed by a short, bald man in a wool tunic with a sword hanging from a thick belt, as well as a tall Indian in a buckskin outfit covered with beaded designs and a headdress made out of a bear's head.

"I'll call the police if you all don't leave this instant!" snarled Mr. Stoop at the lot of them.

Mrs. Stoop huddled behind her husband, already blaming him for allowing her to end her days murdered in a mobile home.

"The police, eh Stoop?" sniffed the elderly

knight. "Very brave of you. Too scared to fight your own battles, eh?"

"Who do you think you are?" shouted Mr. Stoop. "How dare you talk to me like that in my house!"

"You call this a *house*? I've seen bigger bread bins than this."

The younger knight stood between the two men before they came to blows.

"Now, Sir Hector," he said to the old man. "We have been sent here by the king to resolve a conflict."

"I can resolve it right now with cold steel," growled Sir Hector, his hand on the hilt of his sword and the waxed tips of his moustache quivering.

Mrs. Stoop shrieked.

"Sir Hector, you're frightening this good lady," said the younger knight. "Let us introduce ourselves like gentlemen. President Stoop, my name is Sir Amory Swain. This is my commander, Sir Hector Jolly, younger brother of the king and Superior General of the Illustrious Order of Knights of the Blue Sock."

This Sir Amory didn't even notice Mr. Stoop's snub, for his attention was gripped by the vision of Aunt Hazel, who had just wandered out of her bedroom into the family room. Since dinner, she had exchanged her customary black bandana for a black ski cap, which she wore tugged low over her unruly hair. Her electric guitar was strapped to her back like a quiver of arrows.

Oliver was surprised to notice that Sir Amory could not stop looking at her, his eyes glazed as donuts, a lovesick puppy's expression on his face.

"Continue with the introductions, Amory!" stormed Sir Hector.

"Ah yes!" said Sir Amory, still not quite able to take his eyes off Aunt Hazel. "This," he said, motioning to the short bald man, "is King Ole, Lord of the Geats, and this is Chief Albert Negahnquet of the Potawatomi. We are King Evander's war council, and have been sent to you by him to parley."

"I think," said Mr. Stoop to the strange ambassadors, "that you boys have been working too hard down at the costume shop. I recommend a long vacation. And you can start now by *GETTING OUT OF MY HOUSE!*"

Only King Ole flinched at this blast from Mr. Stoop.

"Thank you for bringing up the question of property, Mr. Stoop," smiled Sir Amory. "I can see you're a man who likes to get straight to the point. Are we correct in understanding that you are a president?"

"I am," said Mr. Stoop, straightening his back and lifting up his chin.

"And you are president of an entity called—the Republic of Staplers?"

"I am," repeated Mr. Stoop. "What's it to you?"

"Simply establishing the facts, Mr. Stoop. Now, your claim is that this land is your property?"

"It most certainly is my property."

Sir Hector snorted and muttered, "Pig's swill!"

"You wouldn't happen to have any proof of this claim, Mr. Stoop?" inquired Sir Amory.

"Of course I've got proof," said Mr. Stoop. "I have the *title deed.* And my lawyer will be very happy to show it to your lawyer."

"What do we care, Amory, about some preposterous piece of paper," groused Sir Hector. "The Cow Park belongs to Patria by virtue of the Treaty we signed with Tim Jenkinson."

Mr. Stoop rolled his eyes and sighed.

"And who is "Tim Jenkinson"?

"Did we get the name wrong?" said Sir Amory. "We're not very good at American history. We mean the chappie who was president when we signed the Treaty of Alliance. Jeff Timlinson? Tom Joplinstuff?"

"Thomas Jefferson!" shouted Oliver. Shocked at himself for bursting out, he slunk back towards his tent.

"That's the one," said Sir Amory, pointing at Oliver. "Sonny Jefferton."

"Are you trying to tell me," said Mr. Stoop, a broad, smirk breaking over his face, "that you are from a country called Patria and that you think you own my property because your king signed a Treaty with Thomas Jefferson?"

"Excellent!" smiled Sir Amory. "Got it in one."

"I don't suppose you'd like to show me this Treaty?"

Sir Amory did not have a quick reply to this question. He fumbled for his words, and when he turned to Sir Hector for help he found him studying the toes of his iron boots.

"I'm afraid Mr. Stoop," stammered Sir Amory, "that we cannot show you our Treaty of Alliance with the United States."

"And why not?"

Sir Amory gulped, and then croaked in a small voice.

"Because it's been missing for over two hundred years."

"Beg pardon?" said Mr. Stoop.

"Because it's been missing for over two hundred years!"

Mr. Stoop hooted. A clear, shrill, you-have-got-to-be-kidding-me sort of hoot.

"*Of course* your sole proof has been missing for over two hundred years!"

Oliver wished his father didn't keep making

fun of the ambassadors. Chief Albert kept staring at Mr. Stoop with a simmering expression, as though considering the various recipes he might use to shrink his head.

"And where, may I ask, is this Patria of yours?" chortled Mr. Stoop.

"You're standing in it," replied Sir Amory. "But the village of New Ilion and the castle are about half a mile or so through those woods."

Oliver's eyes bulged. *A secret kingdom only half a mile through the woods!*

Mr. Stoop's eyes bulged too, but for a different reason.

"And you expect me and my family to just pack up our bags and tootle off, because you nutters come into my house with toy swords in your scabbards?"

Sir Hector's eyes narrowed into slits.

"Sir, I will sport with this "toy sword" all over that dog's face of yours!"

King Ole, Lord of the Geats, stepped in to break the tension.

"President Stoop, we are all anxious to learn more about the Republic of Staplers."

Mr. Stoop grunted.

"What sort of work do Staplers do?" inquired King Ole.

Mr. Stoop looked at him as though he were an idiot.

"Pretty much what you'd expect."

"I'm afraid I have no idea what Staplers do, President Stoop."

Mr. Stoop rolled his eyes and replied.

"They hold pieces of paper together with their teeth!"

King Ole stared at Mr. Stoop, not sure of what he had just heard.

"They hold pieces of paper together with their *teeth?*"

"That's what I said."

"I see. Do they perform this work well?"

"Usually," said Mr. Stoop. "But if they act up, you just pull back their heads and shake them."

King Ole looked horrified at his fellow ambassadors.

"King Evander is prepared to reward you handsomely for any inconvenience, Mr. Stoop," said Sir Amory. "Whatever you prefer—a string of ponies? A bronze scarab from the ancient city of Troy? Or perhaps an assortment of gold rings, broaches, and necklaces?"

Mrs. Stoop's head poked out from behind her husband.

"Did you say *gold?*" she asked politely.

"They don't have any gold, my pet," scoffed Mr. Stoop. "Let's not humor these lunatics. Now for the last time, I bought this land with my own hard-earned money, and if you don't leave this instant, I'm going to—"

"And from *whom* did you buy the land?" asked Sir Amory.

Mr. Stoop hesitated.

"I don't know the man's name. A wealthy businessman. I worked with two of his representatives."

"And what were their names?"

"Mr. Blaggard and Mr. Squilch."

"I cannot say I am familiar with those names, Mr. Stoop," said Sir Amory. "I don't believe those are Patrian names."

"What do I care what you believe," cried Mr. Stoop. "For the last time, get out of my house!"

"So you refuse to continue parley?" asked Sir Amory.

"You can take your parley," Mr. Stoop replied, "and stick it in your ear!"

"Excellent," said Sir Hector with a rueful grin. "Let's get back, Amory, and tell King Evander to declare war."

"We are very sorry to disturb you," said Sir Amory to Mr. Stoop. "We will report our parley to King Evander." He then added, with a last longing glance at Aunt Hazel: "We were so hoping to become friends."

"Report away, by all means," said Mr. Stoop.

"And while you're at it, be sure to tell your king I think he's a raving lunatic, too. Nighty-night, you nutcases!"

At the doorstep, Sir Hector turned to Mr. Stoop.

"This isn't the last you've seen of me, Stoop. I'll have you off Patria's land if it's the last thing I do."

"Calm, grandpa. You'll stress your heart."

It took a moment for Sir Amory to restrain his aged friend, but after he had succeeded Oliver flew to the open front door and watched as the two knights clanked behind King Ole and Chief Albert toward the woods.

CHAPTER FIVE
BUBBLES & BURPS

For some time after the embassy had left, Mr. and Mrs. Stoop squabbled over the meaning of this strange visit. Mrs. Stoop wanted Mr. Stoop to ask if she could at least see the gold rings and necklaces the men offered. Mr. Stoop flatly refused.

"They're trying to frighten me off my land," he insisted. "I bet they belong to one of these crazy groups who hate television and frozen food. The next time one of them even *looks* at my property, I'm calling the police."

Mrs. Stoop finally went to bed, but Mr. Stoop was too wound up to sleep. So was Oliver. From a seat on the couch he watched his father peeking through the blinds of one of the family room windows, as if expecting the Patrian army to charge out of the woods at any moment.

"Think I'll do a little recon," Mr. Stoop mumbled to himself.

"What's *recon?*" Oliver asked.

Mr. Stoop was startled by his son's voice. He hadn't realized that Oliver was still there.

"*Reconnaissance?* It means "spying." Secretly gathering information on the enemy. Assessing their resources. Don't you remember? The team and I always do recon on the Indian camp at the beginning of our "Battle of Fort Wayne" sketch."

"So you're going to *spy* on them?" Oliver gasped.

Mr. Stoop studied his son for several long moments.

"I am, Oliver. And you're going with me."

"*Me?*"

"You."

"But, Dad!"

"Yes," Mr. Stoop smiled, nodding his head. "Service to the family, Oliver. Just the kind of discipline you need."

An hour later, Mr. Stoop and Oliver's recon expedition had nearly reached the end of the wide, almost neat path they had been surprised to find in the woods. In the light of full moon, they cut two very strange silhouettes. From the wardrobe of the Midwest War-Historical Re-Enactment Association, Mr. Stoop had dressed himself in a cotton shirt, breeches, and boots. But as Mr. Stoop didn't have any children's costumes, Oliver was forced to wear a pair of men's colonial-era knickers (so long they dragged upon the ground), an old straw hat that his mother used to wear in the garden, and an old flannel shirt of Mr. Stoop's. He felt like a clown. All he was missing was the face paint.

Stepping past the last line of trees, Mr. Stoop and Oliver found themselves on the edge of a wide and gently rolling prairie. And there, nestled in a shallow valley under the glorious moon, was a village. It reminded Oliver of the paper town in his *Pop-Up Book of the Middle Ages*, as though the prairie had opened like the covers of a book to reveal this wonderful surprise inside.

It was a neat little village with narrow streets and houses and shops all huddled together in a circle as if for warmth against the chilly night. While there was fire and gaslight shining from the windows, there was apparently no electricity. And there was not a single car or truck to be seen.

Oliver felt his eye drawn to the north, where he saw, sitting on an island in the middle of an immense moat, a *castle*—no doubt what the "princess" had referred to as the Castle of Patria. It was a real castle, with squat turrets, battlements, and a drawbridge. Because of the moat, the only access to it was by one of two low bridges—one from the north and one from the south—both of which were illuminated by Chinese lanterns strung along the railings.

"Now *that's* the castle I want!" sighed Mr. Stoop.

They had been silent for so long that the sound of his father's exclamation made Oliver jump.

"What is all this, Dad?"

"Heaven knows, son. An amusement park, maybe. That wacky quartet tonight—maybe they were trying to drum up business?"

But Oliver thought it strange that salesmen from an amusement park would go door-to-door so late at night. He also didn't see how people would get to the amusement park; there didn't seem to be any roads from the outside world.

"Come on, Oliver" Mr. Stoop said. "We'll do a little recon anyway. You never know, this still could be the headquarters of some crackpot group. Let's leave the flashlights over here."

Oliver and his father laid their flashlights at the base of an oak tree and began to walk down the slope of the prairie toward the village.

"Are we just going to walk right in?" Oliver asked his father.

"Of course. If it is some kind of "medieval" amusement park, people will think we're employees. If the place turns out to be full of loonies, in these get-ups they'll just take us for inmates."

The central street of the village was called High Street. There were no street signs—the name "High

Street" was painted right on the sides of the houses. As they walked along, Oliver breathed in the smoke from the chimneys that jutted out of every rooftop. The smell was so inviting; it seemed to urge him to knock on one of the doors and ask if he could stretch out his feet before the fire inside.

Toward the center of town they came upon a pleasant, whitewashed building with big baskets of flowers hanging along the wall. The happy sounds of talk and laughter, along with the intoxicating smell of what Oliver guessed was meatloaf, emanated from the opened windows. A brightly-painted sign hanging over the street said, "Bubbles & Burps." Underneath the letters was a picture of a smiling knight in armor hoisting a foamy mug of beer.

"A pub?" wondered Mr. Stoop. "Maybe the park *is* still open. C'mon, Oliver."

Mr. Stoop cracked opened the door of the pub to get a peek inside—which allowed the scratch of a fiddler's melody to dance into the street.

"Just follow my lead, son. We're not going to talk to anyone until I'm sure this is an amusement park."

Oliver followed his father through the crowded pub. All the tables were full of laughing, chattering people, and many more were standing up and talking in groups. It might have been a crowd at the World Cup, for all the different ethnic groups that were represented. Most looked like Americans or Europeans, but others looked like Mexicans, African-Americans, and Potawatomi. Their dress wasn't quite what Oliver would call medieval. Their costumes—if they *were* costumes—looked more like how people dressed at the time of the Revolutionary War. The women wore long dresses with short sleeves, while the men wore coats and breeches. Bonnets and top hats hung from the wooden pegs along the wall.

Dominating the middle of the pub was a large, open fireplace, and nestled closely around the fire were several rocking chairs occupied by old men, most of whom were asleep. The fiddler, who was blind and wore dark glasses, wound his way merrily among the rocking chairs, without bumping into a single one.

Mr. Stoop spied a couple of open stools at the bar. He and Oliver sat down on them and examined the place as they waited for the bartender. Oliver thought it nice that the pub was filled with so many families. But he was alarmed to discover King Ole and his family playing cards at a corner table. Fortunately, the king's back was to the bar. Across from him was a large, muscular woman who looked as though she could take on the entire pub if necessary, and still keep an eye on her hand of cards.

Kids were piled high and deep on both benches of their table, and the whole family was dressed in outfits made of leather and sheepskin with thick leather boots and leather helmets. Even the mother wore a small helmet with two little horns coming out of the sides. From their look, Oliver could only guess that they were, well, *Vikings.*

The bartender approached—a large, ruddy-faced man with sweat dripping down his forehead.

"Ain't had the pleasure of seeing you gentlemen in here before," he smiled. "My name is Mugg. This is my establishment."

"We're just visiting!" laughed Mr. Stoop, as though he had just made a good joke. "Ha! Ha! Ha!"

Mr. Mugg studied them with a squinting eye.

"Visiting? Visitors to Patria are rare indeed."

"We've just come to visit our friend—*the king,*" said Mr. Stoop. "We're very old friends of the king. From a far away land."

Oliver looked away, a little shocked to hear his father tell an outright fib.

"Friends of the king—very honored to meet you, I'm sure!" said Mr. Mugg, smiling again. Then he dropped his voice. "Here on official business, eh? About this ruckus with the invader, I suspect. Is King Evander thinking of forging an alliance with your people? Don't worry. I'll keep it under wraps. I understand you want to enjoy a quiet drink after your journey. So what'll it be? I've got cider, lemonade, or ginger beer for the boy."

"A lemonade for the boy, and a mug of your best ale for me."

"Very good, gentlemen."

And with a conspiratorial wink, Mr. Mugg left to pour their drinks.

"Mystery solved, Oliver," Mr. Stoop smirked. "They're all re-enactors. And not very good ones at that. *'Is King Evander thinking of forging an alliance with your people?'* Give me a break. Totally unconvincing."

Mr. Mugg brought their drinks, but before they could take a drink they were approached by a tall young man in a long brown cassock that reached all the way down to his sandaled feet. He had the weirdest haircut Oliver had ever seen. He was completely bald, except for a narrow band of hair that circled round his head. In his hand was a tray filled with slices of cheese.

"Good even, gentlemen. Like to try our smoked cheddar?"

"Eh? Er—all right," said Mr. Stoop. Oliver took one, too. The smoky flavor was delicious.

"The Cheese Festival, remember, is a week from Sunday," grinned the young man. "Some of our best cheeses in years."

"Oh, I've got it down on the calendar," said Mr.

Stoop, rolling his eyes at Oliver as he munched his cheese.

"It's so pleasant to see everyone having a good time!" beamed the young man. "I haven't been out of my cell this late at night for years."

"Your *cell?*" said Mr. Stoop, swallowing his cheese as though he had just realized it was poisoned.

"Yes. Usually we're locked down in our cells by this time of night. Have either of you seen Brother Aidan? Ah, there he is. We must be getting back. See you at the festival!"

Mr. Stoop huddled close to Oliver.

"*Cells!* I've changed my mind, Oliver—it *is* a loony bin. Can't be a very high security facility, though, if they let all the inmates out for a night at the pub. Probably keeps them under control."

"He kind of looked like a *monk,*" Oliver said, but Mr. Stoop didn't hear him.

"Keep your head down, Oliver. It's that crazy old duffer again."

Oliver looked across the pub to see Sir Hector tacking through the crowd toward the circle of old men by the fire. The suit of armor had been replaced by a long blue tunic with leather boots. But on the breast of the tunic was the same insignia of the silver shield with the blue sock.

A barmaid brought Sir Hector a tankard of ale,

but it did not put him in a happy mood. He kicked one of the old men awake.

"This is the most disgraceful lot ever I clapped eyes upon! An invader is on our doorstep, and all the once noble Knights of the Blue Sock can think to do is take a nap."

"I wasn't napping, I was resting up for the battle," winced the poor old knight who had been kicked.

Sir Hector let out a great guffaw.

"You've no reason to be sore at us, Hector," continued the kicked man. "It's not our fault your brother doesn't take the threat seriously."

"What's the matter, Hector?" called out the large Viking-looking woman from across the pub. "Somebody take your land?" She laughed heartily at her own joke and slammed the table with her fist. "If one of our Geat warriors was king," she continued, "he wouldn't be sitting around worrying about some lost Treaty. He'd march an army out there and take Patria's land back. Right, Ole?"

"Y-y-yes, b-b-b-blossom," replied her husband.

The door to the pub burst open, and Sir Amory clanked in, helmet off but still in his armor. His cheeks were hot and he was breathing so heavily he could hardly speak.

"What is it, Amory?" demanded Sir Hector.

"Stoop…son…here."

"WHAT!?"

Sir Amory struggled to get hold of his breathing.

"So sorry, Hector. I manned my post outside the Stoop's tin hut, just as you ordered me. Then I heard the most exquisite sound! It was her, Hector. *Hazel!* She was playing music on a rather odd-looking lute. And she was singing, Hector. *Singing!* Of course she's musical—dear, sensitive soul. I could hear her through her opened window, with a voice as sweet as a nightingale—"

"AMORY! Stop blithering on about that witch's yodeling. What about Stoop?"

"Yes," Sir Amory huffed. "I was getting to that. Well, I soon realized how hard it is to undertake espionage in a full suit of armor. She heard my clanking outside her window. She poked her head out—and then she spoke to me! *Me,* Hector!"

"She spoke to you? What did she say, you nauseating puppy?"

"She said Stoop and his boy had left for Patria."

"You mean they're coming *here?*"

"Should already *be* here, I would think. Precious Hazel said they were coming to spy on us."

Cries of alarm popped like corn kernels about the room.

"*Knights to arms!*" shouted Sir Hector. "After that Stoop! He and his son are here in Patria!"

There was a great commotion, as many of the

48

knights needed help out of their rocking chairs. Causing even greater confusion was the fact that it had been years since many of the knights had actually taken their swords out of their scabbards. Some swords were stuck so badly it took two or three knights gripping the hilt to pull them free.

Upon hearing Sir Hector's alarm, Mr. Mugg turned to re-examine the foreign man and boy he had served just a little while before.

But their stools were empty.

Mr. Stoop and Oliver had escaped through the swinging door into the kitchen. "Here," Mr. Stoop whispered as he grabbed articles of clothing from pegs on the wall. "Put these on, son."

"But *Dad*—"

"You heard the man, Oliver! They know we're here. Do you want them to catch you and stick you in one of their *cells*? I have to get you out of here— this is a *madhouse!*"

Oliver had no choice but to obey his father and put on the apron and cap. It was no great guess to judge that the apron belonged to Mr. Mugg, as it fitted Oliver as though he were wrapped in a parachute. Mr. Mugg must have been making pies in it recently, for it was covered with what looked and smelled like cherry juice.

Mr. Stoop, meanwhile, donned what was apparently Mrs. Mugg's cotton work dress and bonnet.

"Ready?" he asked.

Oliver shook his head no, but his father ignored him.

There was a mudroom off the kitchen, which in turn led out into the street. Mr. Stoop opened the street door a crack. There was a great commotion outside.

"Keep your head down, Oliver, and follow me."

They popped out the door of the pub and began to scurry through the crowd. Oliver tried to keep his head down, but he couldn't resist one look. He saw an old knight complaining to another that he hadn't even finished his ale. Next to them King Ole's wife was chiding him for not riding out that instant to recapture the Cow Park.

Then Oliver caught a glimpse of a man with stringy, greasy hair darting out of the lamplight into the shadows. He didn't get a good look at the man's face. But he reminded Oliver of—

"This way, son!"

In a motherly way Mr. Stoop gripped Oliver close and led him down an empty street. They hadn't gone a step before disaster struck.

"Stop!"

Mr. Stoop and Oliver shuddered to a halt.

"Stop! No mother and child must venture out alone—not tonight!"

It was Sir Hector hobbling toward them, clearly thinking he was about to rescue one of the female kitchen staff and her young son returning home for the night.

"Do not be afraid, my good lady," he wheezed. "I am here to protect you. There's a mad man abroad. You cannot venture home alone. Allow me to escort you."

"Please leave us," said Mr. Stoop, in a strikingly good imitation of an old dish woman's voice. "My son mangled his hand with a carving knife. I have to get him home."

Sir Hector looked with horror at the "blood" covering Oliver's apron.

"Nonsense!" he cried, taking Mr. Stoop by the shoulders. "I would be pickled with onions before I allowed a defenseless woman and her wounded son to fall prey to the ruffian stalking our land tonight."

"Leave us alone!" Mr. Stoop shrieked as he tried to jerk himself away from Sir Hector.

"Good woman, please! Think of your son—"

"Oh, he's all right!"

"Woman!"

Again Mr. Stoop tried to jerk away from Sir Hector's grip, but when Sir Hector wouldn't let go

Mr. Stoop did something that an old dish woman with a son with a mangled hand most probably would not have done: he slugged Sir Hector in the belly, grabbed Oliver, and ran.

Doubled over in the street, Sir Hector lifted his head and wheezed:

"Stoop!"

CHAPTER SIX
CEASE-FIRE

Oliver woke as to a dream. Swaddled in satin pajamas and satin sheets, he was nestled in the most comfortable bed he had ever slept in. His head lay on a satin pillow made cool by the morning breeze that brushed across his face from the open window beside him.

Where was he?

Scenes from the night before flickered through his memory. Sir Hector and Sir Amory marching him and his father into the castle…being led down to a dungeon and held in a jail cell…his father gripping the bars of the cell and demanding to be allowed to call his lawyer…then, who knows how much later, being woken up and carried upstairs by a monster of a man…satin pajamas waiting upon the pillow…collapsing into this wonderful bed….

Then the blood turned to a freezer pop in his veins. *Was this where they let you sleep the night before your execution?*

Oliver sat up and surveyed his surroundings.

He found himself in no mere bedroom, but an entire apartment. Through a door he saw a room crammed with bookshelves. Another door on his right opened to a small sitting room. A door on his left led to what Oliver dearly hoped was a bathroom.

When he returned Oliver noticed for the first time the enormous oil painting on the wall above his bed. It depicted the Trojan Horse standing amidst the burning city of Troy, a story Oliver knew well from *A Boy's Big Book of Famous Battles*. The ancient Greeks had been at war with the Trojans for years—a war started, for reasons Oliver never could understand, over a girl. Just when it looked like no side would ever win, a crafty Greek warrior named Ulysses came up with a plan to defeat the Trojans once and for all. The Greeks sailed their ships out of sight, pretending to have packed up and gone home. But they had left a huge wooden horse outside the gates of Troy, their little way, it seemed, of saying, "Thanks for the war, boys. No hard feelings. Sincerely, the Greeks." The horse, which had been built on skates, was too big to roll through the gates of the city, so the Trojans had to take the gates off their hinges in order to get the horse inside. That night, Ulysses and his men, who had been hiding in the hollow belly of the horse, snuck out and began wreaking havoc as their Greek comrades poured through the wide-open gates. The Trojans were finished before they were even out of their pajamas.

It was an awesome painting, Oliver thought, but a little dark to have hanging above one's bed. He wondered why it was there.

He was still wondering when Mr. Stoop popped his head inside the room.

"Here you are, Oliver! Quick, change your clothes, strip your sheets and bring them into my room. I have a plan for getting us out of here."

Oliver had just changed back into his clothes when there came a small knock at his door. Not knowing quite what to do, but thinking that the knock sounded friendly enough, he said, "Come in." The door opened and there entered a giant, hairy, vaguely-humanoid figure with stooped shoulders and an impeccably-tailored dark suit.

"King Evander werry much request pleasure of your presence."

Oliver stepped back, startled as much by the size of the creature as by his Russian accent.

"The king?"

"Your father himself as well, most appreciated."

"Uh. My father—isn't quite ready."

"Werry good. Please follow me."

Oliver reckoned that he had better not argue. He followed the creature down the main staircase of the castle and down several long corridors, his entire body rattling with the fear that the king would pronounce a death sentence upon him.

But as soon as he was led into the massive, private study of Evander Jolly IV, King of Patria, Oliver had a feeling that things might not turn out so badly after all.

Still in his robe and slippers, King Evander sat at his desk amid a chaos of books, scrolls, papers and coffee mugs. He was a rumpled old man with wisps of white hair swirling like cotton candy above his shiny bald head. By the way he was gripping a half-gnarled rasher of bacon in his fist while staring with a sickly expression at the wall, it seemed to Oliver that the king was experiencing food poisoning. But, as he eventually would learn, King Evander's distress was much more serious. He was trying to write poetry.

Bustling about the king's desk was a thin, pale man in a dark suit who was attempting to insert some order into the chaos. The giant bowed and lumbered out of the room, leaving Oliver there waiting to be noticed.

"Tell me, Malchio," the king said to the pale man who was now gathering up the king's empty coffee mugs, "do you think *wagon hitch* is a good rhyme for *sandwich?*"

The pale man cleared his throat and offered

what sounded like the usual reply: "I think it an excellent choice, Your Majesty. The Stoop boy is here, Your Majesty."

"Eh? What's that? Boy?"

The king's glassy eye moved from the wall to the man named Malchio and, finally, to Oliver.

"Ah yes. You're perfectly right, Malchio. It's a boy."

The door slammed open and Sir Hector, with Sir Amory at his side, entered the room.

"Where is the father?" Sir Hector grumbled as he glared at Oliver on the way toward his brother's desk. When he and Sir Amory had positioned themselves before the king, Sir Hector continued:

"There was an incident last night, Your Majesty."

"Hm?" replied the king, beginning to gnaw poetically on his rasher of bacon.

"The Stoop Menace—as I predicted to you yesterday—has entered Patria. He and his boy were caught last night spying in the village—*in disguise.*"

"That's very nice, Hector."

The waxed tips of Sir Hector's moustache straightened into exclamation points.

"Listen to me, Evander! I'm telling you there are *spies* in Patria. The President the Republic of Staplers spent the night locked in the dungeons, along with his son."

Oliver thought it best not to correct Sir Hector

as to where he had spent the night.

"*Blast it, Malchio!*" erupted the king as he swatted Malchio's hand away from his papers. "How can I write an epic if you keep coming along and straightening my desk? It shatters the concentration. Why don't you go over in the corner and alphabetize the dust motes?"

"I did a thorough cleaning of the study before Your Majesty came down this morning," smiled Malchio.

"Then go and count the pages of all the books in the library."

"Eighteen million, seven hundred sixty-five thousand, two hundred and thirty-four."

The king squeezed his forehead.

"Then go and make me one of those headache potions of yours. I feel a trying morning coming on."

"Very good, Your Majesty," said Malchio, and retreated with a bow. He padded across the thick carpet, five or six coffee mugs cradled in his arms, and when he came to Oliver he looked at him over his glasses and smiled.

"Master Oliver Stoop, my name is Miching Malchio, King Evander's private secretary. Please be assured that *nearly* everyone in Patria"—he nodded discreetly over his shoulder at Sir Hector and Sir Amory—"would be only *too glad* to let the

Republic of Staplers have the Cow Park. Peace with our neighbors is our one desire."

Oliver nodded his head and said "thank you."

Malchio left the room, but a moment later the door to the study opened again, and a robust, red-haired lady marched in.

"Good morning, Master Oliver," she said, stopping beside him. "I hope you were able to enjoy *some* rest last night. My name is Lady Lavinia. I am Rose and Farnsworth's mother."

She then continued toward the king's desk, making deep impressions in the carpet.

"Good morning, Father," she trumpeted.

"What have I done?" groaned the king automatically.

"Nothing Father—*this* time," smiled Lady Lavinia imperiously as she kissed her father on the head. "I've simply come in to wish you good morning—and to find out what sort of nonsense my uncle has been feeding you for breakfast. Stories about spies and invaders, no doubt."

The waxed tips of Sir Hector's moustache bristled indignantly.

"Uncle Hector," declared Lady Lavinia, "by your recklessness, you have placed our entire kingdom in an embarrassing and, might I add, dangerous situation. Do you know, Father, that last night your brother tried to lock a visiting dignitary, and a president no less, in the dungeons—*with his child?*

"I didn't just try," Sir Hector protested. "I succeeded."

Lady Lavinia repelled this remark with hooded eyelids and a cunning smile.

"For a brief time," she acknowledged. "Until I freed them and settled them into two of the guest suites upstairs."

Sir Hector's face, ruddy even when its seas were calm, exploded into a storm of reds, blues and purples.

"You *freed* them!"

"I freed them. It was outrageous of you, Uncle, to treat our new neighbors in this fashion."

"Did you call them *neighbors!?*" spluttered Sir Hector.

"I did," replied Lady Lavinia. "And we should be doing all we can to welcome them." She smiled at Oliver. "I think that Master Oliver will make a fine chum for Farnsworth."

"*Chum!*" said Sir Hector, choking on the word as though it were a chicken bone wedged in his throat. "They were in *disguise, spying* in the village!"

"Pish," jeered his niece. "They were simply having a look around."

"You mean to say," said Sir Hector, struggling for the words. "You mean to say, that you *believe* that cunning Stoop?"

"And why shouldn't I?" said Lady Lavinia.

Oliver had never seen such a glorious shade of purple as he now observed in Sir Hector's face.

"What about the fact that he's commandeered land that rightfully belongs to Patria?"

"It has long been a question whether the Cow Park actually belongs to Patria, Uncle, as you well know," returned Lady Lavinia. "Mr. Stoop claims to have a legal right to that property, and I see no reason why we should contest his claim. It's not such a very large piece of land anyway, and we should be glad to have such a noble soul as our neighbor. Don't you think so, Father?"

"Eh? What? Whatever you say, my dear Lavinia."

"*Brother!*" moaned Sir Hector. "A foreign power has invaded Patria. You must do something!"

"I must? Well, quite right, Hector. No doubt I must."

But before the king could slip back into his poetic slumber, there came a small knock at the study door. The giant entered and announced that two ladies desired an audience with the king.

"Who are they, Sasquatch?" demanded Lady Lavinia.

"A Meesez Stoop, m'lady," said the giant. "And her seester, Meez Hazel."

Before Oliver could process the fact that the giant's name was Sasquatch, his mother and Aunt Hazel entered the room.

"Good morning!" sang Mrs. Stoop as she flitted into the room like a happy poodle. She carried a large bag of fast food and a plastic bottle of soda. "I'm Phoebe Stoop. This is my baby sister, Hazel. We're your new neighbors. Oh! Hello, Oliver. What are you doing here?"

"It is an honor to meet you both," said Lady Lavinia as she curtsied before Mrs. Stoop and Aunt Hazel. "How kind of you to call."

"Don't you just *love* that!" Mrs. Stoop turned to her sister. "They never break character."

"I should hope not," smiled Lady Lavinia proudly.

The king's daughter then did the duty of introductions. When it came time for him to be formally introduced to Aunt Hazel, Sir Hector, still suspecting her to be a witch, slid behind Sir Amory for protection. Sir Amory blushed like a schoolboy and made odd gargling sounds. Aunt Hazel looked at Sir Amory as though he were a fungus growing in a corner of the shower and adjusted the earphones connected to her portable music device.

"We couldn't wait to come over and say how tickled we are to have you as our neighbors!" gushed Mrs. Stoop. "So we went into town this morning and brought you something from Burger Land. I'm afraid it's not hot anymore, though—can you pop it in the micro?"

"I suppose they've invaded Burger Land, too," lamented Sir Hector to Sir Amory.

"We're so glad you've come," smiled Lady Lavinia, taking the bag of fast food from Mrs. Stoop while trying not to show her disgust. The bottom of the bag was a pool of grease. She went to the door and called for Sasquatch, to whom she gave orders and the bag.

When she returned she bid everyone to take a seat. Oliver took a seat on a couch next to his mother.

"You must have been so worried about your husband and son, Mrs. Stoop," said Lady Lavinia.

Mrs. Stoop blinked her violet-colored eyelids, bewildered by the remark.

"Not to worry. They slept safe and comfortably, I hope, in two of our guest suites upstairs."

Mrs. Stoop looked at Oliver.

"You mean Reginald and Oliver have been *here?*" she said.

"Yes," replied Lady Lavinia. "You didn't notice that they weren't in the house?"

"I hardly notice Reginald from one month to the next," said Mrs. Stoop, bursting into a spree of giggles. "I suppose it was unusually quiet this morning. Anyway, glad they're safe."

As no one was quite sure what to say next, Lady Lavinia launched into a stirring account of the events of the night before, an account accompanied by a variety of snorts from Sir Hector. Mrs. Stoop only half-listened to the story, wondering instead what had happened to the breakfast. Presently, Sasquatch entered bearing a silver tray laden with the goodies Mrs. Stoop had brought from Burger Land.

"Isn't this nice!" said Mrs. Stoop, unable to take her eyes off the man-mountain setting down the tray. "I thought I'd try their new Omelette in a Cup. These three here are Denvers, those are Bacon, Ham and Sausage—I got a couple without gravy for anyone like me who's watching her waist line— and these here are Five Cheese. Oh, and look Hazel! He replaced the sporks with real silverware!"

Sasquatch bowed and stalked out of the room.

None of the Patrians knew quite what to do. The fact that something resembling breakfast had been dumped inside a cup completely befuddled them.

"And that thoughtful Hazel," said Mrs. Stoop, with particular attention to Sir Amory, "didn't let me forget the Hash Brown Balls." Sir Amory followed Mrs. Stoop's finger to the Hash Brown Balls that Sasquatch had placed in a small silver tureen. Mrs. Stoop popped one into her mouth with delight, but the Patrians felt a little sickened by the grease glistening on her fingertips.

"*Sooo* yummy. I don't know how to stop eating them!"

There followed several awkward moments as the Stoop sisters tucked into their cold omelettes and the Patrians did their best to copy them without actually eating anything. Sir Amory was the exception. In an attempt to impress Aunt Hazel, he brought a forkful of Five Cheese Omelette in a Cup to his mouth. But Sir Hector stayed his arm.

"Don't even dream of putting anything of that woman's victuals into your mouth."

"I understand, Mrs. Stoop, that your husband rules the Republic of Staplers?" said Lady Lavinia as she set her uneaten Denver Omelette in a Cup back onto the coffee table.

"Like a tyrant!" replied Mrs. Stoop as she gobbled her Bacon, Ham and Sausage with No Gravy.

At this, the waxed tips of Sir Hector's moustache slashed like rapiers.

"A *tyrant* you say?" stuttered Lady Lavinia.

"You didn't hear it from me," said Mrs. Stoop in a hushed voice, "but I don't think he always treats his people very well."

Sir Hector glanced at his niece with an expression that said, "Will you believe me *now?*" But Lady

Lavinia ignored him.

"How did the land come into your husband's possession, Mrs. Stoop?"

"Oh, it was a *steal!* Absolute *robbery* what we got it for. But if there's anyone who knows how to hoodwink someone into a deal, it's Reginald!"

Sir Hector glanced at his niece again, this time with an expression that said, "Not only are these people usurpers and thieves, they're proud of it!" But Lady Lavinia, though more troubled by Mrs. Stoop's replies than she cared to let on to her uncle, pressed on with a wide, artificial smile.

"But your husband does have a perfectly *legal* right to his land, does he not, Mrs. Stoop?"

"Oh, it's legal all right," Mrs. Stoop replied, batting any worries away with a wave of her hand. "Reginald doesn't floss his teeth without an army of lawyers present."

Now it was Lady Lavinia's turn to glance at her uncle, with an expression that said, "*Now* are you ready to concede defeat, you old poop?"

It was at this point in the conversation that, in the room straight above, Mr. Stoop's escape plan reached its thrilling climax. It was Mr. Stoop's idea to anchor a rope of bedsheets to the leg of his bed and shimmy down to the ground. Now, as Oliver watched through the window behind King Evander's desk, Mr. Stoop was in mid-shimmy. But what Mr. Stoop had not counted on was the brown wiener dog frolicking in the garden. Seeing Mr. Stoop hanging from the bedsheets, the micro-sized hellhound leapt and sank his mini-fangs into Mr. Stoop's ankle.

"Why there's Reginald now!" cried Mrs. Stoop, seeing her husband through the window howling in pain.

All the Patrians turned to see Mr. Stoop twisting about the bedsheet with his ankle clenched between the junior-jaws of the wiener.

In a matter of moments, Sir Hector and Sir Amory had captured Mr. Stoop and escorted him into the king's study.

"What were you *doing* out there, Reginald?" Mrs. Stoop, flustered with embarrassment, asked her husband as he entered the room.

"Locked myself in my room," smiled Mr. Stoop. "Ha! Ha! Ha! Silly of me."

"What a pleasure to meet you, Mr. President," said Lady Lavinia as she curtsied before Mr. Stoop. "I believe our two families are going to be great friends!"

Mr. Stoop gave her a salute, better pleased with this form of insanity than the other kinds he had so far witnessed in Patria.

Sir Hector took the opportunity to whisper into his brother's ear.

"Stake your claim to the Cow Park, Evander! Now is the time to strike!"

"I'm sure I speak for my father," said Lady Lavinia, "when I say how much the entire royal family of Patria would be honored if your family would join us for dinner this Sunday. Don't you agree, Father?"

"Eh?" replied King Evander, who had half of his brother's nose in his ear.

"That would be lovely," answered Mrs. Stoop, as both her husband and Sir Hector looked at her with horror.

"Evander!" hissed Sir Hector into his brother's ear. "Get a hold of yourself, man. You can't entertain these *land robbers!"*

King Evander looked bug-eyed at his brother, then at his daughter.

"May I suggest a cease-fire, Your Majesty?"

These words were spoken by Malchio, returning to the room with the king's headache potion.

"Excellent notion, Malchio," smiled Lady Lavinia. "A cease-fire is just the thing until we can get all this sorted out. And in the meanwhile," she said turning to Mrs. Stoop, "we would be delighted to have your Oliver stay with us. I'm sure he and my Farnsworth will get along famously."

Oliver looked anxiously at his mother, begging her with his eyes to say no.

"That would be *marvelous*," tittered Mrs. Stoop. Then she added, with a sly glance at Sir Amory. "I don't think Hazel has plans for the weekend, either."

Oliver turned to his father, thinking that certainly *he* wouldn't leave him here alone.

"*Dad!*"

But Mr. Stoop took his son's arm and led him, under the watchful eye of Sir Hector, into a corner of the study.

"I don't *want* to do a sleepover," said Oliver, bouncing with fear.

"I know, son," said Mr. Stoop. "But the thing is, you could do some more recon for me."

"*No, Dad—*"

"Oliver, I need to know what's going on in this place so I can tell my lawyer. Here, take my cell phone. I want you to take pictures of everything—but for heaven's sake don't let them see you doing it. Call if there's any trouble."

"But *Dad—!*"

"Oliver would *love* to stay!" Mr. Stoop spun around and announced to the room.

"Excellent," smiled Lady Lavinia. "I'll send Sasquatch 'round for his things directly."

CHAPTER SEVEN
TALE OF THE TROJAN TUB

There are few events in the life of a kid as exciting as a sleepover. The pillow fights, the giggling, the waking up after three hours' sleep feeling like a bank safe has been strapped to one's head. Yet Oliver had never been to a sleepover before—at least not to an *entire* sleepover. Once, a few years back, he had been invited to a sleepover at the house of a kid he barely knew, Curtis Fleen, a frail, ghostly child with a continuously runny nose and ears that looked like they had been modeled on the handles of an ancient Greek amphora. But the whole thing ended in disaster. Oliver got so creeped out in the middle of Curtis's movie selection, *Revenge of the Killer Cockroaches*, that Mrs. Fleen had to call Mrs. Stoop to come take him home.

It was just that Oliver didn't like the thought of going to sleep in a strange bed in a strange house. Sure, he wanted to see Patria, he was dying to discover what it was all about. But he didn't want to *stay* there, not *alone*. As he said goodbye to his mother and father, he felt as though someone were trying to make one of those dog-shaped balloon figures out of his stomach. It would be hard enough, even now, to spend one night at Curtis Fleen's. But a *two*-nighter, at a castle in a mysterious hidden kingdom, and with a kid who wanted to *scalp* him only the day before? The very thought of it made Oliver feel sick.

Then there was the spying his father wanted him to do. How was he going to take pictures and sneak around when Sir Hector, who was already suspicious that Oliver was an enemy spy, would probably be tailing him the entire weekend?

"Mother said that I was to take you out riding," announced Farnsworth to Oliver as Oliver stood in the main doorway of the castle, watching his parents cross the moat bridge. Farnsworth didn't look too happy about the assignment, and Oliver sure didn't like the fact that he was still packing his strange air gun.

"What is that thing?" he asked.

"This?" said Farnsworth, holding up the weapon with a cocky smile. "This is the Magna-Pneumatic Whizzing Biscuit Blaster. I made it myself, with a little help from my father."

"Why does it shoot biscuits?"

"Because my sister's biscuits make great ammunition. She's trying to learn how to cook at her school, Madame Mimi's Well-Ordered School for Ill-Mannered Girls. Luckily for me, though, she can cook about as well as those people from Burger Land."

"I wish you'd put it away," said Oliver underneath his breath.

"Not a chance," said Farnsworth. "You've been caught spying in Patria. Who knows what you'll try next?"

"I don't know how to ride a horse anyway," Oliver said as they came to the stables.

"Who said anything about a horse?"

The Royal Stables of Patria are just to the west of the castle, in a large stone building with a roof of red slate. Farnsworth ushered Oliver through the front doors as his brown wiener dog, Slobberchops, the same monster that had foiled Mr. Stoop's getaway plan, scooted in front of him.

It was dark and cool inside the stables, and the air was sweet with hay. Oliver followed Farnsworth past the rows of spacious stalls, most of which were occupied by horses. Slobberchops bounced all around barking orders at the noble animals, who blinked back at him with bored expressions.

"I don't start my Squire Formation Course until the autumn," grumbled Farnsworth. "So I'm stuck with kiddie stuff."

Farnsworth stopped in front of an extra-large stall at the end of the row. Inside it, covered by a tarp, was something that looked like a car.

"Promise not to laugh," Farnsworth said.

"Promise," said Oliver.

Farnsworth pulled off the tarp to reveal an old car that shone as though it had just rolled off the production line. It had a maroon chassis, a collapsible roof, and a glass windscreen.

"I know that car!" Oliver shouted with delight. He had seen pictures of it, at least, in *A Boy's Big Book of Cars*. For years, every morning at breakfast, he had read that book, memorizing the makes and models of all the cars. Before him was a 1916 Studebaker Touring Car, made by the Studebaker Brothers Company over in South Bend.

"How did you—?"

"It was found in an abandoned barn a long time ago," Farnsworth explained. "It was my grandfather's when he was a boy. He gave it to me for my fifth birthday."

"And you get to *drive* it?"

"*Get* to? I hate it."

"Hate it? This is one of the most famous cars in history!"

"It's for *kids*. I'd rather ride a horse."

"But you get to drive *this*, with the engine on

and everything?"

"Anyone can drive one of these," Farnsworth said. "Crank it up, step on the pedal, and off you go. No skill required."

The groom took a break from cleaning out a nearby stall and helped Farnsworth and Oliver push the Studebaker outside. Farnsworth climbed into the black leather driver's seat while Oliver took the seat beside him. Slobberchops jumped in between them, turning mad circles in excitement.

"Don't go too fast," said Oliver, it suddenly having occurred to him that Farnsworth's driving abilities might not be all one wished for.

"Fast? I can crawl faster than this old crate."

Farnsworth pulled the choke and turned the key to the ignition. Oliver jumped as a small explosion occurred underneath his feet. The car emitted several loud coughs before the engine turned over and began to idle comfortably. Farnsworth pushed the gear shift, stepped on the accelerator, and they were off.

The groom waved goodbye with a smile. They headed west at about fifteen miles per hour.

"I feel like a baby," Farnsworth said.

But Oliver felt exhilarated.

"This is fanTAStic!"

As Farnsworth continued to scowl and grumble about not even *needing* riding lessons, Oliver took in the beauty of the rolling meadow. A ways ahead the woods picked up again, and Oliver could see teepees, and among the trees some simple bark huts in the shape of bread loaves.

"That's the Potawatomi Camp," Farnsworth pointed out. "The boys in the tribe can't wait for the war to begin."

"I remember," said Oliver, the hairs on his head beginning to prickle. "But you don't think there's still going to be a war, do you?"

"There'd better be. What else am I supposed to do with you all weekend?"

Oliver wanted to say, "Why don't we just try to have some fun?" But he didn't want to be scoffed at.

Since Farnsworth, however, seemed so intent on war, Oliver did at least want to clear up the confusion about the Republic of Staplers.

"The Republic of Staplers is not the name of a *land*, by the way, it's just the name of the place my dad works. We're citizens of the United States."

"But your father told Sir Hector and Sir Amory that he was a president."

"Yes," said Oliver, a little exasperated, "but that means something different for us."

"And you said he's building a *castle*."

"Yes, but—"

"And Sir Hector says, anyone who lays claim

to a patch of land and builds a castle on it, takes himself to be lord of that land. That's how it is here in Patria. There are lots of farms and houses about, but only one castle."

Oliver gave up.

Farnsworth, meanwhile, put the Studebaker in park at the crest of the hill near the Potawatomi Camp. Looking back, they had a magnificent view of the village of New Ilion awash in the bright morning sun. It was market day, and the populace all seemed to be out in the central square, buzzing about the stalls filled with fruits, vegetables, and meats.

The thought of food made Oliver think to ask:

"Are those *monks* who make the cheese for the Cheese Festival?"

"Yes. From St. Brendan's Monastery. Over there—"

Farnsworth pointed toward the bell tower of a large monastery on the far side of a river.

"That river is the Fluvius Bubalus. It's Latin for "Buffalo River.""

"Latin?"

"Latin used to be our official language. But when the monks arrived from Ireland everyone liked the way they talked, so English kind of took over."

"When did the monks come?"

"They came over with St. Brendan—520 A.D."

"520? Columbus didn't come until 1492!"

"Who's Columbus?"

While Oliver struggled to take all this in, he noticed a wooden fortress upriver from the monastery. Farnsworth told him that it was the village of a Viking tribe, the Geats.

"*Vikings!*" murmured Oliver to himself.

"The Geats have some of the most vicious warriors in Patria," said Farnsworth. "And the men aren't bad, either. Your father is going to be sorry when he has to face them."

Farnsworth's threats aside, Oliver was absolutely amazed by everything he saw. A tiny kingdom, right in the middle of Indiana, that almost no one in the world knew about. Oliver could hardly comprehend it.

"How long has Patria been here?" he asked.

"I don't know," said Farnsworth. "Thousands of years."

"Stop pulling my leg," Oliver said.

"I'm not even touching your leg."

"*Thousands* of years?"

"Something like that," Farnsworth replied. "Our people came here after the fall of Troy."

Oliver looked at Farnsworth to gauge whether or not he was kidding.

"*The fall of Troy?*"

"You know about Troy, don't you? The ancient

war between the Greeks and Trojans?"

"Sure." Oliver, it will be remembered, had read all about it in *A Boy's Big Book of Famous Battles.*

"Troy is where we all came from," Farnsworth said.

"What do you mean?"

"I mean we're Trojans, originally. Our ancestors sailed here from Troy in the Trojan Horse."

"*In* the Trojan Horse? How do you sail *in* a horse?"

"Easy. After the Greeks tricked us with the Trojan Horse, some of our ancestors who survived used the horse to build a boat. It was huge, you know, and hollow—turned upside down and sliced across the middle, it made for a great hull. No use wasting all that good wood."

Crazy as all this sounded, it at least explained the painting on the wall above the bed in Oliver's suite.

Farnsworth put the Studebaker in gear again, and with Oliver working the pedals, and Slobberchops yipping merrily, they circled back to the castle.

As they rumbled across the rolling meadow, they came upon a colossal oak tree, its ancient limbs sagging so close to the ground they looked like the swirling tentacles of an octopus. Farnsworth brought the Studebaker to a halt.

"Come over here," he said sharply, "I want to show you something."

He led Oliver to a bronze plaque embedded in a boulder a few feet from the base of the tree. Farnsworth said defiantly:

"This is where the Treaty was signed that *proves* the Cow Park belongs to Patria."

Oliver read the legend written on the plaque:

COUNCIL OAK

ON OCTOBER 20, 1808, IN THE SHADE OF THIS OAK, KING PRIAM THE GREAT OF PATRIA (1743-1829) AND UNITED STATES AMBASSADOR ODYSSEUS MURGATROYD (1753-1808), MET TO SIGN THE TREATY OF ALLIANCE BETWEEN PATRIA AND THE UNITED STATES OF AMERICA...

"Odysseus Murgatroyd!" gasped Oliver.

"Yes," nodded Farnsworth.

"You mean he was *real?*"

"What do you mean real?"

"I mean living, breathing, outside the pages of a book!"

"Of course. Why wouldn't he be real? Odysseus Murgatroyd was the first American to discover Patria."

Oliver looked at Farnsworth, waiting for him to

burst out laughing and say it was all a joke.

"You're *serious?*"

"Absolutely. Why wouldn't I be?"

"I just thought he was a character from books."

"There are books?"

"*The Chronicles of Odysseus Murgatroyd, Adventurer.*"

"Never heard of them."

Of all the things Oliver had experienced in the last several hours, this struck him as the most extraordinary: the tall tales he had read in the *Chronicles* were not quite so tall after all.

"So whatever happened to the Treaty?" he asked. "I mean, how did it get lost?"

"You didn't read about it in the *Chronicles* you mention?" asked Farnsworth in return.

"No," replied Oliver. "I haven't read any stories about Odysseus Murgatroyd in Patria. Though I still have a few more to go."

"Well then," said Farnsworth with a heavy sigh. "You'd better come with me to the library."

CHAPTER EIGHT

A SNAKE IN THE GRASS

With the groom's help, Farnsworth parked the Studebaker back in the stables, and then led Oliver into the castle library—a mammoth room with floor-to-ceiling bookshelves stuffed with tomes, papyrus scrolls, and stacks of parchment. On the floor, besides desks and some comfy chairs, were statues and display cases filled with more books, documents, and artifacts from Patria's history.

But the most fascinating object in the library was the wooden ship that dominated the center of the room.

"Hello there!"

Oliver looked up to find, high in a corner, a man seated on a chair fastened onto a rail that ran along the length of the bookshelves.

"Come to see the Tub, eh boys? Hold on, I'll be right down."

"That's my father," said Farnsworth proudly. "He designed that chair himself. Watch!"

Attached to the chair was a steel cable by which it was connected to one of several other steel cables that criss-crossed the library high above their heads. Oliver's fear of heights was so terrible that he could hardly watch as Farnsworth's father, by flipping a latch, disconnected his chair from the rail and pushed off. His chair then gently glided along the cable over their heads to the wall nearest to Oliver and Farnsworth, where a ladder awaited.

"My father likes easy access to the books," Farnsworth explained.

"What does your father do?" Oliver asked as Farnsworth's father hurried down the ladder.

Farnsworth took a deep breath.

"He's a farmer, philosopher, biologist, inventor, mathematician, carpenter, painter, musician—and a swell puppeteer. Did I get it all, Father?"

"Most of it, Farnie. Now, this must be Master Oliver. Lady Lavinia told me you were staying the weekend. Professor Victor Vesuvius, at your service."

He was Farnsworth all grown up, but with a scroll in his hand rather than a Magna-Pneumatic. He had wild sandy hair and was dressed in a long, unbelted scarlet robe with a little matching tam. At first Oliver was puzzled by his last name, but then he remembered that Farnsworth's mother, not his father, was related to King Evander Jolly.

"I hope Farnie is obeying the cease-fire?" said Professor Vesuvius to Oliver, but with a wary glance at his son. "He's a little too keen to prove himself, Farnie is."

Not knowing quite what to say to this, Oliver smiled politely and looked around at all the books.

"It's a marvelous collection, isn't it?" swelled Professor Vesuvius. "Most of the scrolls came from the ancient Library of Alexandria in Egypt. Wonderful story how they got here—"

Farnsworth gave his father a desperate look.

"Ah. Yes. But that story can wait. Master Oliver probably wants to see the Tub."

"Actually, Father—" began Farnsworth.

But Professor Vesuvius was already off. He led them over to the massive vessel, which reminded Oliver of drawings he had seen of Noah's Ark. It had one large door in the middle of the hull, and a strip of small, circular windows running down its length. Its figurehead was the neck and head of a horse, its mouth wide open, which made the horse look as though it were charging into battle as it galloped across the sea.

Oliver suddenly remembered something he had read in *A Boy's Big Book of Ancient Rome*. He asked Professor Vesuvius:

"Didn't a warrior named Aeneas escape from Troy and sail with some of his men to Italy?"

"You're absolutely right, Oliver," said Professor Vesuvius. "Aeneas was a Trojan warrior who founded what was to become, eventually, the Roman Empire. It's all told in an epic poem called the *Aeneid* by a chap named Virgil. But don't get King Evander started on *him*. He thinks he's a hack of the first water."

"But then *other* Trojans escaped and sailed here to America?"

"That's right. Their original plan was to join Aeneas. But they sailed a toucher off course, and the next thing they knew they were out in the middle of the Atlantic, heading this way. Good thing they packed extra sandwiches. They nearly starved to death."

Oliver couldn't believe what he was looking at. *The Trojan Horse*—turned upside down!

"This isn't the real thing, of course," said Professor Vesuvius. "It's been over three thousand years since the first Patrians left the shores of windy Troy. Not much remains of the original vessel save for a few broken planks that we keep in that case over there. What you see here is a three-quarter sized replica, based upon pictures found on ancient Patrian pottery, as well as what we read about the tub in the *Patriad*, Part 1."

Professor Vesuvius led them over to a display

case where some scraps of the original hull were kept. After looking at these for a moment, he drifted over to a wax figure of a jolly old man wearing a crown and a majestical robe. At the base of the figure was a plaque with the words:

KING PRIAM THE GREAT OF PATRIA
1743-1829

In the figure's right hand was a replica of parchment, on which was written:

TREATY OF ALLIANCE
BETWEEN THE SOVEREIGN KINGDOM
OF PATRIA &
THE UNITED STATES OF AMERICA
OCTOBER 20, 1808

"That's a very old wax figure of King Priam, Master Oliver," said Professor Vesuvius. "King Priam is one of King Evander's ancestors. But understand, the throne of Patria isn't always held by a Jolly. We *elect* our kings. It's just that we happen to like Jollys. They hate being king, which makes them just perfect for the job. That wax figure is an excellent likeness of old Priam. He himself posed for it, over two hundred years ago. Same goes for this one here."

Professor Vesuvius pointed to another wax figure next to King Priam.

"This is—"

"—Odysseus Murgatroyd," finished Oliver.

"Master Oliver has heard all about him," explained Farnsworth to his father. "There are books about him in the Republic of Staplers."

"Is that so?" said Professor Vesuvius. "Books?"

Oliver couldn't stop staring at the figure of Odysseus Murgatroyd. Since, like King Priam, Murgatroyd himself had posed for it, Oliver figured it must be as good a likeness of the heroic woodsman as was likely to exist. The figure was dressed in buckskin pants and shirt, and sported Odysseus's trademark coonskin cap. It also had the long golden hair draping down the back and shoulders that Oliver had read about in the *Chronicles.*

But it was the wax figure's eyes that most fascinated Oliver. They were made out of something that looked to Oliver like bright, blue marbles, and looked so real that Oliver expected the figure to wink at him at any moment.

"Odysseus Murgatroyd was a brave man," said Professor Vesuvius. "And a good friend of Patria. His death was a great blow to King Priam."

"Death?" said Oliver.

"You wanted to know what happened to the

Treaty," said Farnsworth, glaring at Oliver as he used the Magna-Pneumatic to point down the way to a diorama of wax figures.

The diorama was a death scene—with wax figures looking much newer than the ones Oliver had already seen. Odysseus Murgatroyd lay on the ground, a wound in his side. A figure that looked like King Priam bent over him, a wax tear running down his cheek. And a third figure, a tall man with broad shoulders and a full, black beard, dressed in what Oliver now knew as the uniform of the Knights of the Blue Sock, bent over Odysseus Murgatroyd on his other side. Behind the scene was a painted background of the castle library itself.

At the base of the diorama was a plaque:

THE DEATH OF ODYSSEUS MURGATROYD

"We learned all about it in school," said Farnsworth. "Odysseus Murgatoryd was the first American to discover Patria. He went and told your president, Toby Jeppington—"

"Thomas Jefferson," corrected Oliver.

"Right. Anyway, Jiffyspoon sent Odysseus Murgatroyd back to Patria as his ambassador, directing him to sign a Treaty of Alliance with us, so that we could all live together in peace."

"Unfortunately," continued Professor Vesuvius,

"right after the signing ceremony, raiders attacked the signing party that was gathered at the Council Oak. Americans, I'm sorry to say. King Priam got away to safety, but Odysseus Murgatroyd was killed."

After all those close scrapes with British soldiers, grizzly bears, raging rapids, and unfriendly Comanches, Odysseus Murgatroyd's glorious career had ended here: in the castle library in Patria. Oliver felt oddly sad: Odysseus Murgatroyd had seemed to spring to life just moments before, and now, already, he was dead.

"In the attack," continued Professor Vesuvius, "Odysseus hid Patria's copy of the Treaty, but unfortunately for all of us, he wasn't able to tell anyone where he hid it before he died."

"What about Turkey Beard?" asked Oliver. "Where was he in all this?"

"Turkey Beard!" said Farnsworth, his face contorting as though he had just swallowed a bite of one of his sister's biscuits. "That snake in the grass!"

"Snake in the grass?"

"He betrayed Patria," snarled Farnsworth. "He *killed* Odysseus Murgatroyd. He was in cahoots with those American raiders."

"*What?*" said Oliver, dumbfounded. He couldn't believe that *Turkey Beard*, the most loyal scout in the history of scouting, was being accused of such treachery.

"That man there was an eyewitness," said Professor Vesuvius.

Professor Vesuvius pointed to the broad-shouldered knight in the diorama. "That's Sir Mycroft Malchio, one of the greatest knights in Patria's history."

"*Mycroft* Malchio?" repeated Oliver. "You mean—?"

"Yes," smiled Professor Vesuvius. "The revered ancestor of King Evander's private secretary."

"But why?" Oliver said. "Why would Turkey Beard want to do such a thing?"

"Money," said Professor Vesuvius. "The band of American raiders didn't like the idea of Patria existing right in the middle of the United States, and they paid Turkey Beard to help them do away with Odysseus Murgatroyd."

Impossible, thought Oliver, though he realized he didn't have much evidence to support his feeling.

"This doesn't sound like the Turkey Beard I know from the *Chronicles*," he said quietly.

"What are these *Chronicles,* Master Oliver?" asked Professor Vesuvius.

"*The Chronicles of Odysseus Murgatroyd, As Narrated by His Faithful Potawatomi Scout, Turkey Beard.* It's a series of adventure stories. At least, I thought they were stories."

"Tell me, Master Oliver," said Professor Vesuvius, narrowing one eye, "who did you say wrote these *Chronicles*?"

Oliver realized that, as the author of the *Chronicles*, Turkey Beard could make up any story he wanted.

"I don't want to disappoint you, Master Oliver," said the professor, "but we Patrians believe that Turkey Beard was responsible for betraying both his friend, Odysseus Murgatroyd, and the good people of Patria."

"A snake in the grass," repeated Farnsworth.

CHAPTER NINE

THE LAST WORDS OF ODYSSEUS MURGATROYD

L ady Lavinia suggested that Farnsworth enjoy lunch with his guest down in the summerhouse, followed by a swim in the lake.

"Haven't I done enough consorting with the enemy?" complained Farnsworth to his mother. In return, Lady Lavinia tweaked her son on the nose and told him that he'd better be a good host to Oliver or he could say goodbye to the Squire Formation Course.

Oliver didn't feel like spending any more time with Farnsworth than Farnsworth did with him. But with a pat on the head from Lady Lavinia he went up to his suite to change into his swim trunks— which Mrs. Stoop, alerted by Lady Lavinia, had packed in the bag of clothes and toilet articles she had given to Sasquatch to bring back to the castle.

Like a water hazard on a golf course, the lake is located in the middle of the greensward just to the east of the castle. After getting changed Oliver walked down alone, and it was a good thing too. For as soon as he caught sight of Farnsworth standing on the pier in his swim trunks, he had to bite into his towel so that Farnsworth couldn't hear him laughing.

Farnsworth's swim trunks were, well, unusual. To Oliver, they looked like a pair of baggy long johns, canary yellow with orange circles splattered all over them.

To Farnsworth, however, Oliver looked just as ridiculous.

"I see you Staplerians like to swim in your underwear!" he laughed merrily.

Princess Rose joined Farnsworth and Oliver at the lake, and if Oliver thought Farnsworth's swim trunks were weird, they were bland compared to the get-up in which Rose came down to the lake. She wore a long, rose-and-white striped dress complete with a sailor's collar and kerchief, a matching hat, rose-colored leggings, and rose-colored shoes. Even her towel was rose.

By the time they all arrived at the summerhouse, Sasquatch had set out a magnificent-looking lunch of cold fried chicken, potato salad, baked beans, corn on the cob, and lemonade—with a ham bone for Slobberchops.

"Farnie," said Rose to her brother, "I asked Sasquatch to bring down some of my biscuits, but he said you had eaten them all. I'm glad you find them so scrumptious, but you've been going through them like candy."

Oliver noticed Farnsworth trying to hide a mischievous grin. His sister clearly had no idea that her culinary efforts were chiefly serving to build up her brother's arsenal.

Several kids from New Ilion joined them after lunch, and they spent the afternoon playing "Greeks & Trojans" on the large wooden rafts that Sasquatch brought out of the nearby boathouse. Rose insisted upon being Andromache, "the most beautiful woman in Troy," with Oliver as her brave and glorious husband, the Trojan hero Hector. It was great fun, Oliver thought, as long as he kept out of the way of Farnsworth, who was a little too eager to toss "Trojans" into the water. It was only when Rose called out to him in her Andromache voice to catch her before she "swooned"—as she did about every two minutes—that Oliver wished he were back in his tent with a book.

But as Oliver dried himself off at the end of the day, his mind drifted back, as it had been doing all afternoon, to the disturbing revelation of the morning. He just couldn't believe what Farnsworth and Professor Vesuvius had told him about Turkey Beard. Would a trusted scout, whose own life had been saved any number of times by Odysseus

Murgatroyd—as, for example, in "Irritations Among the Iroquois"—turn on that same friend and all the people of Patria? It didn't seem possible.

Then again, as Professor Vesuvius said, Turkey Beard was the author of the *Chronicles*. Maybe everything he had written was a lie?

As they walked back to the castle, Farnsworth sped several paces ahead of Oliver and pretended as though he wasn't there. Oliver was sick and tired of his rudeness, and part of him was glad not to have to talk to him. But another part of him wanted to tell Farnsworth what he was thinking.

"There are still several stories in the last volume of the *Chronicles* I haven't read," Oliver blurted out. "I'd sure like to know if Turkey Beard wrote anything about the day the Treaty was signed. Maybe he said something about where Odysseus Murgatroyd hid the Treaty?"

Farnsworth stopped and turned to Oliver.

"How can you believe anything he wrote?"

"I can't prove it. But I just don't think Turkey Beard would do such a thing."

"But Sir Mycroft Malchio *saw* him kill Odysseus Murgatroyd! It's in the *Patriad*."

"I can't explain that," Oliver admitted. "I just have faith in Turkey Beard. Why don't we go back to my house and get the last volume of the *Chronicles*? Who knows? Maybe Turkey Beard gives a clue about the whereabouts of the Treaty. We could end up discovering where it's really hidden."

Oliver had said this last bit with a small giggle, not really believing that they could ever find the missing Treaty.

But the words struck Farnsworth in a very different way.

"You mean a *quest!*" he burst out.

"I don't know," said Oliver. "I suppose."

Then Farnsworth's face, which had lit up with excitement, clouded over again.

"Why would *you* be interested in finding the missing Treaty? No matter where it's hidden, it says that the Cow Park belongs to Patria."

"Don't you get it?" said Oliver impatiently. "I don't care about the Cow Park. I'd just like to find out the truth, and if I can, keep my father from getting himself killed. I also wouldn't mind clearing Turkey Beard's name. Not that I think we have much chance of finding the Treaty. It's just a wild idea—"

"A quest!" proclaimed Farnsworth. "To find the long lost Treaty of Alliance between Patria and the United States! If we succeed, we'll have done something no one has done *in over two hundred years.* We'll finally settle the question of who owns the Cow Park. We'll be *heroes!* And, I'll get to skip the "Quest" portion of the Squire Formation Course."

Farnsworth took a long look at Oliver.

"But we can't go fetch the *Chronicles* tonight," he said.

"Why not?" asked Oliver.

"Come with me and I'll tell you."

So to his happy surprise Oliver found himself in a cease-fire, if not a full-blown friendship, with Farnsworth Vesuvius. Before dinner, in fact, Farnsworth took Oliver in to see King Evander, as he wanted to tell his grandfather all about their quest. The boys found King Evander sitting cross-legged on the floor of his study brooding over a map of Patria painted on a large square canvas. Spread across the map were groups of small, painted tin figures—Patrians, Potawatomi, Geats, even monks from St. Brendan's holding tiny platters of cheese.

"What are you doing, Grandfather?" said Farnsworth as they entered the study. "Making battle plans?"

"Eh? Battle plans? No, no, Farnie. I'm leaving all the battle plans to your great-uncle Hector. The map and tin figures here help me to visualize the action in my new epic poem."

"*New* epic poem? What happened to your old epic poem?"

"Boring, Farnie! No one wants to hear about

"The Almost Civil War with the Geats of 1932." So the Geats threatened to secede from Patria when the referee failed to award them a penalty in the soccer championship against the Knights of the Blue Sock. No doubt they should have been awarded a penalty. Quite robbed, I daresay. But is that subject matter for great poetry? I think not."

"So what are you going to write about, Grandfather?"

A twinkle appeared in the ancient monarch's eye.

"The Great, Momentous War Between Patria and the Republic of Staplers!"

"Speaking of which," Farnsworth said, "Oliver and I are going on a quest to clear Turkey Beard's name and find the Treaty."

"Are you really?" said the king as he moved the tin figures of Sir Hector and Sir Amory next to the thimble which served as the Stoop mobile home.

Farnsworth went on to explain to King Evander how he and Oliver were going in the morning to fetch the last volume of the *Chronicles* and hopefully find the key to the mystery of where Odysseus Murgatroyd hid the Treaty.

When he was finished, the king wished the boys God's speed and assured them that he would portray their heroic virtues with all due embellishment in his poem.

"And Malchio—"

"Yes, Your Majesty?"

Oliver turned around, surprised to find the super-secretary standing right behind them. He hadn't even heard him come in.

"I want you to draw up a list of rhymes for the names Farnsworth and Oliver."

"Very good, Your Majesty. May I immediately suggest, for Master Farnsworth, *yarn's worth, barn's dirt, and darn squirt?* "

It was the rule at the castle that everyone put on their best clothes for dinner, and when Oliver went up to change he found a suit of evening clothes hanging over a dressing stand next to his bed. Dinner itself was like dinner in a royal palace. Indeed, it *was* dinner in a royal palace, consisting of several courses, each of which Oliver found more delicious than the last. Oliver cleaned every plate put in front of him, being ravenous after an afternoon swimming in the hot sun.

When the last spoonful of pudding was dispatched the family assembled on the patio at the top of one of the castle towers, which afforded a magnificent view of New Ilion in the summer twilight. There stories and jokes were told, stories and jokes Oliver would have enjoyed more thoroughly if Princess Rose and her own sleepover guest, a girl with the improbable name of Cheerily Chatterbox, had not insinuated themselves into the seats next to him. They kept whispering together in a soul-sickening way, and after each whisper Cheerily's freckled face would turn the color of a blood orange as she snorted and giggled in Oliver's direction.

Oliver didn't have a book to read in bed, but he was glad to find a copy of the *Patriad*, Part 14 in the small bookroom of his suite. Eagerly he turned the pages to the account of what happened on the day the Treaty was signed:

The company clustered for oaths under oak:
King Priam the Great, sun-glint off his crown,
and Odysseus Murgatroyd, the awesome ambassador,
standing in for President Tom Joffreytown.
Witnesses watched as signatures were scribbled:
Lord Gorm of the Geats and Abbot Finbar,
along with wise William, Potawatomi chieftain,
and a bevy of Blue Socks to serve as king's guard.
The Treaty was signed on two pale parchment copies,
two copies forever set apart to survive,
one to remain in the Patrian stronghold,
the other in the United States National Archives.
But alas! Fate foreknew the ceremony spoiled!
The alliance to launch with disruption and dread.
As over the greensward grim raiders rode,
their rifles a-ringing and spitting out lead.

What were they after, these battling bandits?
What did they want from a party of peace?
"They want the alliance," realized wise Odysseus,
"they want to destroy our brand new Treaty."
A courier had come with Odysseus from Washington,
a messenger with a pinto as pronto as wind;
whose task was to take back the Treaty to T.J.
and announce that the U.S. and Patria were friends.
"Take this copy," Odysseus ordered this gofer,
"and ride on to Washington, District of C.,
tell ol' T.J. we had us a ruckus,
but the Treaty's been signed by both Priam and me."
Amid hailstones of lead the go-between galloped,
with one pirate pursuing on a demon nag,
until Lord Gorm lobbed a dagger most deftly
and plunked that pirate in the small of the back.
The Treaty was signed on two pale parchment copies,
one went with the messenger, one stayed behind,
gripped in the glove of the cunning Odysseus
who planned to hide it where no one could find.
"I'll keep it safe," he said to King Priam.
"Not one of these brutes will touch it, no way.
It would take far more than this horde of hooligans
To crush the alliance that was forged here today."
"Now away! Away with the king!" yelled Odysseus,
to Sir Mycroft who swiftly obeyed the command.
The broad-shouldered Blue Sock, his body a bulwark,
protected the prince of our once-peaceful land.
With the monarch mounted on the Malchio mare,
as the bullet-storm rained, though each drop falling short,
the Blue Sock succeeded in sheltering his sovereign,
escorting him into the keep of his fort.

Back at the old oak, noble and gnarled,
the peace party reformed as a fighting force,
and held off the hijackers with flintlocks and pistols,
not to mention a couple of Viking broadswords.
The wily woodsman, not once ever doubted
the unswerving allegiance of his steadfast aide;
not once did it ever enter his noggin:
his long-faithful scout was to blame for the raid.
For Turkey Beard conspired to conceal the hijackers,
Supply them with steeds and shrapnel to shoot;
It was Turkey Beard who swore to deliver Odysseus
In exchange for some cattle and a wad of fresh loot.

Oliver ran his eye down over the next few pages, hoping against hope that the poem would say *something* about where Odysseus Murgatroyd hid the Treaty. But it didn't. The poem went on to describe how the raiders were finally defeated when some Geat women, hanging out the wash down in their village, caught sight of the raiders and ran over and dragged them down off their horses with their bare hands and pummeled them. Then the scene shifted to the castle library, the very library that Oliver had visited that morning, where Sir Mycroft Malchio came upon Turkey Beard trying to force Odysseus to tell him where he hid the Treaty.

But the woodsman refused to leak the location
of where he had tucked the Treaty away.

So the scout with a murderous look in his eye
brandished a blade—his old friend to slay.
Sir Mycroft cried "Stop!" as he raced to assist,
which had an effect that turned him to jelly—
for when Odysseus looked to see who had shouted
Turkey Beard's blade found a place in his belly.

Oliver looked up from the book and smashed a tear crawling out of the corner of his eye. He couldn't bear to read the next lines closely—which described Turkey Beard's flight from the castle. But when he came upon the very last lines of that section of the poem—the report of Odysseus Murgatroyd's final words—he took a deep breath and read them slowly:

King Priam arrived as his friend was fading,
his bold-breath leaving, his strength nearly spent;
his shaking hands seizing Sir Mycroft's lapel
as if for the life that had now all but went.
The monarch knelt down and blessed the brave ranger,
as his grateful tears now abundantly flowed;
and begged of Odysseus one last commission
to tell where the Treaty of Alliance was stowed.
With the very last breath that Odysseus mustered
he uttered the words of a deep mystery:
said to King Priam as his soul took its leaving:
"You will always, my friend, find an ally in me."

Chapter Ten

Operation Indigo

Oliver and Farnsworth couldn't go back to the mobile home that night to get the last volume of the *Chronicles*, because Farnsworth had another important plan already in motion: Operation Indigo.

"Flying Squirrel's granny makes the indigo dyes for all Patria," Farnsworth had explained that afternoon as they walked back to the castle. "Flying Squirrel promised to get me a vial of the stuff—which we're going to pick up at the Potawatomi Camp tonight. We will then return to the castle, where I will apply the indigo in generous doses to the hide of Rose's poodle, Cassandra. In the morning we will be awakened by Rose's horrific screams, and our happiness will be complete!"

Oliver suspected that Princess Rose would do more than just scream when she discovered the results of Operation Indigo. But he hoped—*prayed*—that as an only partly-willing guest he would be spared the worst of her counter-attack.

The operation went into effect precisely at midnight, when Sasquatch hauled Farnsworth out of bed with one huge, hairy hand. Waking to find himself several feet off the floor in the clutches of the gi-normous butler, Farnsworth hollered bloody murder before Sasquatch's free hand slammed like a gate over his mouth. It was a good thing that Rose and Cheerily Chatterbox were in Rose's suite on the opposite side of the castle boisterously singing tunes from their favorite band of minstrels, The Earwigs, or else Operation Indigo would have finished before it started.

With the full moon floating upwards through the sky like a lost balloon, Farnsworth and Oliver crept across the moat bridge before breaking into a jog up the sloping greensward in the direction of the Potawatomi Camp.

It was half past midnight by the time they got there, but they found the whole tribe still very much awake, sitting around a crackling bonfire constructed in the open area in the center of the camp. Oliver stared in amazement at them all. He knew there were Native Americans living all over the United States, but he didn't know any still lived like *this*: in bark huts and teepees, with the men and boys in buckskin outfits, painted faces, and headdresses, and the women and girls in long buckskin dresses adorned with colored beads and flowers. But then again, Oliver had to keep reminding himself: this wasn't the United States. This was Patria.

It was a party, apparently. A succulent smell of meat—from a deer being roasted on a spit—made Oliver want to eat dinner all over again. There was entertainment, too. A tall, wiry Indian in a colorful, beaded poncho appeared to be performing some kind of one-man show. He stood alone in the midst of the tribe performing a story, and it was clear from his grand gestures and passionate expressions that he was very much in the moment.

Farnsworth threw a pebble at the back of Flying Squirrel's head, and Flying Squirrel snuck over to where they were waiting beyond the ring of fire. Oliver was glad to see Flying Squirrel without a bear knife in his hand.

"A Storyteller arrived this afternoon," whispered Flying Squirrel. "We've never had a visit from this one before. Sorry you can't stay. He's telling stories that can't be told outside the tribe."

"No problem," whispered Farnsworth. "We're just here for the indigo."

"Indigo!"

Flying Squirrel slapped his forehead.

"You didn't *forget?*"

"Sorry, Farnsworth! I'll get you some tomorrow."

"But I need it now!"

"Granny will be on to me if I try to sneak away in front of everyone. Besides, I want to hear the story."

"How long till it's over?"

"He's only telling us a short story tonight. He should be done by breakfast."

"Breakfast!"

Farnsworth was about to explain that Operation Indigo was worth any amount of mortal danger when their conversation was interrupted by a very formal, not to say snooty, voice with a British accent.

"I beg your pardon, boys. Is my performance falling below my usual *electrifying* standards?"

It was the Storyteller. He peered into the shadows at the three boys as though he wouldn't have minded if they were taken into the woods and shot.

The Storyteller was certainly not what Oliver imagined a Potawatomi storyteller to be like. He would have expected an ancient-looking man with a brown face as worn as an old baseball mitt and clear, sky-blue eyes that looked as though they had witnessed everything since the Mastodons roamed North America. Instead, here was a very modern-seeming man with a British accent and a snippy manner, who clearly didn't appreciate sharing the limelight—or the bonfire, as the case may be.

"Thank you for the interruption," he continued, with about a gallon of sarcasm in his voice. "I mean, there's nothing like having one's performance *destroyed* right when one is getting to the *very best part.* But why should you respect my craft? I only studied *three years* at the Royal Academy of Dramatic Arts in London. I only spent *five years* with the Royal Shakespeare Company. *I only played Romeo in Verona itself!*"

The Storyteller broke off. He bowed his head and clutched his face as though suffering from a migraine headache. The tribe looked on, mesmerized.

"Why does he have a British accent?" Farnsworth whispered to Flying Squirrel. Flying Squirrel shrugged and whispered back:

"He's from Michigan, actually. But he studied acting in England, and it kind of went to his head."

The Storyteller removed his hand and shook his head.

"Sorry," he said. "It's gone. My focus lies *shattered in the dust.* I can no longer continue with this tale."

The tribe groaned.

The man Oliver knew as Chief Albert, now in a magnificent feather headdress, stood up and motioned to the boys to come into the circle.

What sort of torture did the Potawatomi reserve,

Oliver wondered, for non-tribal members who interrupted their stories?

Hiding a few feet behind Flying Squirrel and Farnsworth, Oliver slunk into the circle, his heart in his mouth.

"Good evening, Prince Farnsworth," bowed Chief Albert. "So good of you to think of joining us tonight. I suppose your mother thinks you're fast asleep in bed?"

The tribe laughed, and in the glow of the fire Oliver saw a grin spread across Farnsworth's face.

"I'm sorry to interrupt the story, Chief Albert," Farnsworth said, with a twitch of his head in the direction of the Storyteller.

"I would like to meet your friend," said Chief Albert, and Oliver was relieved to see him smiling at him. "Formally, that is."

Farnsworth turned and motioned for Oliver to come forward.

"Master Oliver Stoop," said Farnsworth, "I would like you to meet Chief Albert Negahnquet of the Potawatomi."

Oliver didn't know quite what to do, so he bowed deeply from the waist. The tribe burst into laughter, but the chief motioned with his hands for them to knock it off.

"Let us hope there will be peace between our lands, Master Oliver," said Chief Albert. "Tell me, do you know anything of the ways of the Potawatomi?"

Oliver didn't know what to say. The entire tribe was waiting for him to say something intelligent. Then a thought jumped into his mind.

"I know about Turkey Beard!" he blurted out.

A woman gasped. The Storyteller fell backward in surprise. Out of the corner of his eye Oliver saw Farnsworth look away, apparently in embarrassment.

"Turkey Beard!" exclaimed the chief. "Strange you should mention that name. You know of Turkey Beard, Master Oliver?"

"Why did I say that?" Oliver chastised himself. *"Now I've offended the whole tribe."*

"Most Patrians believe Turkey Beard to have been a traitor to their kingdom," said the chief solemnly.

Oliver glanced at Farnsworth and saw him chewing on his thumb knuckle.

He then took a deep breath and said:

"I-I don't believe he was a traitor, sir."

The chief cocked his head and looked at Oliver with great amazement. Then he turned to the Storyteller.

"Tell me, Storyteller. Do you know any tale of our Potawatomi ancestor, Turkey Beard?"

"Me? Most Honorable Chief, I—I—don't think I

can tell any more stories tonight. My concentration is simply—*obliterated!*"

Clutching his forehead, the Storyteller began to stagger out of the circle of firelight—though not without a glance at Oliver with deep resentment in his eyes.

"What a night!" sighed Farnsworth as, half an hour later, they crept up the central staircase of the castle. "No indigo...mad Storyteller. Want some chocolate? I have a stash underneath my mattress."

Yet the cruelest blow of the night was still to come. As soon as they entered Farnsworth's chambers Farnsworth let out a scream as though the ghost of Turkey Beard himself was waiting for him under his bed. But it was, if possible, an even more gruesome horror. For there, lying fast asleep on Farnsworth's bed, was Slobberchops—dyed indigo from snout to feet.

CHAPTER ELEVEN

A YELLER-BELLIED SNEAK ATTACK

Breakfast the next morning featured blueberry pancakes and sausages, but it was nonetheless a subdued affair. Not only because Oliver and Farnsworth were exhausted from being up half the night, but because Farnsworth was still sulking over what Princess Rose had done to poor Slobberchops. The whole ordeal had made Farnsworth lose his appetite: he was only able to manage six pancakes and five sausages, with just two scoopfuls of scrambled eggs. Feeling terrible for what his micro-hound had to suffer, Farnsworth even let the purplish victim sit on his lap and gobble as many sausages as he liked.

"I spared you, Master Oliver," Princess Rose smiled archly as she and Cheerily joined the boys in the breakfast room. "I'm sure you were only being polite in going along with Farnsworth's nasty scheme."

"Where did you get that indigo?" Farnsworth hissed at his sister.

But she wasn't telling. She only bounced giddily in her chair and exchanged giggles with Cheerily.

"So," said Rose, "are we going to the Republic of Staplers to fetch the last volume of the *Chronicles* right after breakfast?"

"How did you hear about the quest?" demanded Farnsworth.

"Grandfather told me. You didn't expect to go without me, did you Farnie? Cheerily would be going, too, but she has to get back home and re-do her pigtails."

Cheerily erupted into a flurry of snorts and her freckled face once again turned the color of a blood orange.

"You're not going anywhere," said Farnsworth. "Girls don't go on quests!"

This earned Farnsworth a swat on the side of the head.

"You're not allowed into the Wyvern Weald, remember?"

"Grandfather lets me go."

"Grandfather would let you challenge a Geat warrior to a wrestling match."

"But you went into the Weald with me the other day!"

"That was before I realized you were going on a quest. Quests are notorious for their danger."

"I shouldn't be surprised by your tactics,"

Farnsworth grumbled. "A girl who will dye a dog indigo will stop at nothing."

Oliver and Farnsworth departed the castle right after breakfast, each of them anxious to find out whether the last volume of the *Chronicles* shed any light on what happened to the Treaty and the reputation of Turkey Beard. As they walked the mile through the woods, Farnsworth explained to Oliver the origin of the name "Wyvern Weald."

"It means "Dragon Forest.""

"Dragon Forest?" said Oliver.

"Centuries ago, a Blue Sock name Sir Wynkyn claimed to have seen a dragon in this forest. No one much believed him. But every day he would ride out here to do battle with the dragon, and every night he would return home without seeing so much as a garden snake. He became quite a laughingstock. The forest was named the Wyvern Weald as a joke."

"I was reading the *Patriad*, Part 14 last night," said Oliver, "and it said, during the raid at the Council Oak, a messenger escaped to Washington, D.C. with the U.S. copy of the Treaty. If that's so, then why doesn't King Evander ask the President of the United States to make him a copy of the Treaty?"

"It's been tried," said Farnsworth. "But every time our ambassadors get close to the president's house, soldiers threaten to throw them in jail."

Remembering the Patrian Embassy from two nights before, Oliver could pretty easily see why.

As they continued on, Oliver felt himself dreading coming to the end of the woods. How would his father react when he showed up at the mobile home with Farnsworth? Would he think he was fraternizing with the enemy? No doubt he would try to get Oliver aside and demand to know the results of his "spying." What would he, Oliver, say? That he got sidetracked by a quest for the missing Treaty of Alliance between Patria and the United States? That would go over beautifully.

As they began to come out of the woods into the field Patrians knew as the Cow Park, Oliver let out a groan when he saw, huddled in front of the mobile home, the twenty-or-so members of the Midwest War-Historical Re-Enactment Association. But curiously, he didn't see his father among them.

"Is that your father's army?" asked Farnsworth.

"Not really. They just pretend."

"They don't look like they're pretending," observed Farnsworth.

Farnsworth had said this with good reason. The Midwest War-Historicals were clearly not their usual sluggish selves on the morning of a practice. Oliver could hear angry shouts and bickering.

"Master Oliver!"

Startled, Oliver and Farnsworth turned to

find a section of the bracken along the edge of the Weald quivering with strong emotion. Then there appeared the head of Sir Amory Swain.

"What are you *doing* there, Sir Amory?" said Farnsworth.

The dull lovesick gleam in Sir Amory's eye grew even duller.

"Like a deer panting for water, I am awaiting a glimpse of the fair Hazel. Not to mention doing a little spying by order of Sir Hector. Oh! I hope you don't mind, Master Oliver!"

"No, I guess not," said Oliver, who, in a spirit of fair play, thought he should admit that he was supposed to be doing some spying, too. But before he could say anything Sir Amory held out to him a piece of folded parchment.

"Master Oliver, would you be so kind as to give this to your Aunt Hazel?" He blushed. "It's just a little poem I wrote. It's not finished, but you might be my only chance to communicate with her. Tell her I'm sorry that I couldn't think of a rhyme for "Hazel." That is, except for "nasal." But I didn't want to write that."

Oliver took the note as Sir Amory disappeared behind the bush again with a grateful sigh.

"Your daddy's been tryin' to get you on the phone all morning!" barked one of the War-Historicals at Oliver as the boys approached the muster of troops in front of the mobile home.

This was Pete, Mr. Stoop's top "lieutenant." Pete wore a brand new replica American uniform from the French and Indian Wars, though three of the shiny brass buttons had to remain unbuttoned over his bulging belly.

Bill (short for Mabel), stood next to Pete. She was Pete's mother-in-law and at eighty the oldest member of the team. She wore a buckskin outfit and her grey hair in a ponytail such that she looked, Oliver thought, like Odysseus Murgatroyd's grandmother. She had been in the re-enacting game for nigh on thirty years and was the quickest musket-loader in the entire membership of the Midwest War-Historical Re-Enactment Association—and she was legally blind in one eye.

From Bill's musket came a sharp metal click, and she spoke in a voice with the consistency of burnt molasses:

"You'd better git yesself in there, boy. There's been a yeller-bellied sneak attack. The chief is waitin' on your report."

Bill then cast her one good eye on Farnsworth.

"Looks like you got yesself a prisoner. Want me to thow 'im in the utility shed?"

"No!" cried Oliver. "He's not a prisoner. He's an—an ambassador. Ambassadors can't be made prisoners of war."

"I told you they weren't pretending!" Farnsworth said hotly as Oliver took him aside. "I knew I should've brought the Magna-Pneumatic!"

"Just take a walk to the far side of the field," Oliver said. "I'll be out in five minutes."

Oliver pushed past the members of the team and opened the door to the mobile home. What he saw hit him like a punch in the face. Drawers were pulled out and emptied onto the floor. Furniture was overturned. The contents of the refrigerator—eggs, tomatoes, milk, mayonnaise—had been tossed about everywhere.

The place had been robbed!

Oliver went to where his tent lay flat upon the floor. He managed to find the door flap and crawled inside. His sleeping bag and pillow and reading flashlight were still there. But he didn't see his collection of the *Chronicles*.

He crawled back outside and began poking around the debris in the family room, but the books were nowhere to be found.

"Oliver!"

Mr. Stoop stormed into the room with the air of an Icelandic volcano just seconds from blowing its stack. "Why couldn't I get through to you on the phone?"

"I don't know, Dad. I tried last night before I went to bed, but I don't think they have cell phone reception in Patria. Have you seen my *Chronicles of Odysseus Murgatroyd?*"

"Your *what*? How can I think of children's books at a time like this? Look at this place, Oliver! Those thieving madmen broke into our home last night while your mother and I and Aunt Hazel were out to dinner. And that's not all. Oh, no! *They kidnapped the Lawn Beast.*"

Oliver thought he detected the glint of a tear in his father's eye.

"My poor Lawn Beast!" whimpered Mr. Stoop. "Those crackpots had better not harm her! Now Oliver, tell me what you've learned."

Knowing that he couldn't avoid answering the question, Oliver thought he'd at least try to do his best by Patria.

"Patria's really great, Dad. We took a tour yesterday in Farnsworth's Studebaker—a *real* Studebaker. And you won't believe it, but there's a village of Vikings. *Vikings*, Dad. And then we went for a—"

"This is no time for *Travel the World with Oliver Stoop.* What I need is inside information about those fiends—especially that geezer Hector."

"Sir Hector is pretty all right, Dad. I mean, I haven't seen him do anything really suspicious."

"That's because he's been over here making a shambles of my house. Look, Oliver. Eggs and tomatoes and mayonnaise everywhere! They clearly just wanted to mess the place up out of spite."

Oliver couldn't deny it. No ordinary thief splashes mayonnaise on a TV screen.

"But how do we know someone from Patria did all this?" Oliver said desperately.

"Come on, Oliver!" wailed Mr. Stoop. "You're as bad as your mother. All she and your aunt can think to do in a crisis is go off shopping. Tell me, who else could have done it? There's no other human being for miles."

Oliver didn't have a reply for this.

"If we could only find the Treaty," he said quietly, "that would solve everything."

"Don't let them brainwash you, son! There's no Treaty. These people have been playing dress-up for too long. Do you really think that Thomas Jefferson signed a treaty with the ancestors of those wackos?"

Mr. Stoop threw open the door and went out to rejoin the team. Oliver, not quite knowing what he was going to do, hurried down the corridor and placed Sir Amory's poem on the pillow of Aunt Hazel's bed. Then he went back outside to make sure Bill hadn't arrested Farnsworth.

He found his father standing in front of the troops, shaking his fist in the direction of Patria.

"YOU CAN'T INTIMIDATE ME, YOU

THIEVING FRUITCAKES! YOU HAVEN'T YET HEARD FROM THE MIDWEST WAR-HISTORICAL RE-ENACTMENT ASSOCIATION!"

There were loud cheers from the troops. Bill fired her musket into the air and everyone hit the decks.

"No more play-actin'," she growled and aimed a gleeful spit in the direction of Patria. "We got ourselves a *real* war on!"

Oliver found himself running toward the Weald before he even knew he had made a decision.

"See you later, Dad! I'm going back to the sleepover."

"Oliver!" shouted Mr. Stoop. "Come back! I don't want you going back there!"

But Oliver didn't stop. When Farnsworth saw him he cut across the field to join him, and together they disappeared into the woods.

Meanwhile, the satellite once again making its turn some two hundred miles above Mr. Stoop's balding head automatically began taking pictures. The satellite delivered these images electronically to a computer sitting on the desk of one of the most powerful persons in the United States government: the Secretary of Defense.

A buzzer sounded from the secretary's

computer. He put down the report he was reading and looked at his computer screen. A moment later an image popped up of the Western Hemisphere as seen from two hundred miles in space. In the lower right-hand corner of the screen was an image of a control stick. The secretary double-clicked his mouse on the stick, and then it was as if he, sitting there at his desk in Washington, D.C., moved from a position in outer space down, down, down toward the Earth, zooming in toward a small red box encompassing a rural portion of north central Indiana.

A series of black and white satellite photos appeared on screen, stacked one on top of the other like a deck of cards. With his mouse the secretary was able to look at one photo and then sweep it away in order to look at the next.

Even though they were taken from outer space, all the photos showed, pretty clearly, a bird's-eye view of a large piece of rural property. The secretary had seen photos of this property many times before, but never introduced by an alarm. Using the virtual control stick, the secretary zoomed in on one particular photo. And sure enough, he soon found out what prompted the alarm. On one end of the property was what looked like a mobile home with several cars parked outside of it and maybe fifteen or twenty people huddled together.

"Good gravy!" muttered the secretary. "Those aren't Patrians!" He pressed a button on his phone.

"Connie, get me the president!"

CHAPTER TWELVE
WHAT TURKEY BEARD SAW

Y ou think the *Chronicles* were *stolen?*"
Farnsworth huffed as he and Oliver, now
hidden in the Weald, slowed down to a
walk.

"A thief—or thieves—broke into our mobile
home last night," said Oliver. "They stole my
father's lawn mower. They probably stole the
Chronicles, too. I had nine books inside my tent, and
all nine of them are gone."

"It couldn't have been anyone from Patria," said
Farnsworth. "None of our people have even heard
of the *Chronicles*."

Oliver didn't want to say aloud that, since the
previous day, Professor Vesuvius knew about
them, along with Chief Albert, not to mention the
king! Any one of them might have told Sir Hector,
who might have ordered Sir Amory to carry out the
theft.

Farnsworth suggested that after lunch in the
summerhouse they take another swim. They were

still eating the meal that Sasquatch had brought down when Rose entered the summerhouse, a self-satisfied smile on her face.

"And what do you want?" said Farnsworth.

"It's what *you* want," Rose said, and from behind her back she pulled out the final volume of the *Chronicles of Odysseus Murgatroyd*.

"*Where did you get that!*" cried Oliver.

"Your mother must have placed it in your overnight bag," Rose laughed, "thinking you would want something to read at bedtime. And when Sasquatch unpacked your bag for you, he placed it on one of the bedside tables in your suite. That's where I found Dogsbody reading it."

"Dogsbody?" said Farnsworth.

"He told me he was asked to clean the windows in Master Oliver's suite this morning. He saw the book on the bedside table and couldn't resist picking it up. I found him reading it after breakfast this morning when I came upstairs to look for you. I came up to ask you one last time to let me go with you on the quest. But you were already gone."

Oliver had never seen the book on his bedside table. But there were, in fact, two bedside tables in his suite, one on each side of the bed, and he guessed Sasquatch had placed the *Chronicles* on the one on the far side of the bed. Oliver had been too engrossed the night before in the *Patriad*, Part 14 to notice.

"Now may I join you on the quest?" Rose asked politely, but there was a tone to her voice that said that if they didn't say yes, she would throw both of them, and the book, into the lake.

Oliver and Farnsworth looked at one another.

"We obviously can't do it without you," Oliver smiled.

"It's three for the questing," said Farnsworth, more grudgingly.

Rose beamed and handed the book to Oliver. He took it and opened it up to the Table of Contents. He ran his eye quickly down to the final stories in the book, the ones he hadn't yet read. The titles of the last two stories made him catch his breath with excitement:

Chapter IX
In Which We Discover a Tiny, Unknown Kingdom

and:

Chapter X
In Which We Spend a Season in Patria

Oliver and Farnsworth then told Rose all about the break-in at the mobile home, and how someone else in Patria was looking for these stories in the

Chronicles.

"We have to be careful not to tell anyone that we have the book in our possession," warned Farnsworth.

"Will you read the stories out to us, please, Master Oliver?" asked Rose as she snatched the unbitten leg of chicken out of Farnsworth's hand and sat down. Oliver happily began flipping through the pages of the book, trying to find a spot that might say something about the hidden Treaty. He read aloud from Chapter X, though he didn't try to do Turkey Beard's voice:

King Priam invited Odysseus and me to spend the rest of the summer in Patria, an invitation we were both eager to accept. While Odysseus took up residence within the castle walls, I enjoyed the hospitality offered by my people, the Potawatomi, whose camp can be found along the line of woods at the northernmost part of this strange but very welcoming kingdom.

Oliver looked up from the book. Through the windows of the summerhouse he could see the same castle of which Turkey Beard wrote sitting splendidly before him, and, just over the rise of the greensward, he could see the same tops of the trees under which Turkey Beard stayed with the Potawatomi. If he had read this chapter three days earlier, Oliver would have thought it was just a wonderful tall tale. But looking now at the very landscape that Turkey Beard was describing, he felt his chest swell at the thought that what he was reading about was *real*.

The next several paragraphs contained detailed descriptions of Patria, including a reference to the "Chase of Chatterbox."

"Ah!" Rose smiled. "Cheerily will be so proud."

But both Oliver and his audience grew restless as Turkey Beard went on and on with descriptions of the flowers, plants and animals of Patria. Clearly he was writing for readers who would have no chance of ever seeing the place, but it was rather dull for those seeking in those pages clues to a great mystery.

"I'm going to skip forward, if you don't mind," Oliver said.

"Please do," munched Farnsworth.

Oliver scanned the pages of the next and last Patria story for any mention of the Treaty. He found none. In fact, one of the few passages he found involving *people* was a passage in which Turkey Beard described Odysseus Murgatroyd's friendship with King Priam. Oliver read:

Odysseus and King Priam quickly became good friends, as they shared a love of clever wordplay. Their conversation was littered with all manner of puns and riddles.

One night a cow wandered into the castle and was found chewing upon the pages of poetry strewn upon the floor of King Priam's private study.

*"This is an **udder** disaster," declared Odysseus.*

*"I wonder what sort of **beef** he has with my poetry?" returned the king.*

*"I don't know if I've **heifer** seen a sadder sight," volleyed Odysseus, as he collapsed giggling into the king's arms.*

It only got worse from there.

One afternoon, while the King and Odysseus were playing Boa-Wickets on the greensward—a strange game in which balls are rolled under the legs of cows—King Priam asked his guest, "Who's ready for ice cream?" To which Odysseus replied, "Why sure!" At which King Priam tipped his head back and screamed like a man who has just walked into a bear trap.

"Get it?" he cried, tears of laughter running down his sun-burnt cheeks. "Who's ready for I SCREAM?"

"Helen's Nose!" groused Rose. "This isn't getting us anywhere."

"That's pretty much the end of the chapter," said Oliver.

"HA!" barked Farnsworth. "I get it! 'Who's ready for I SCREAM?'"

While Farnsworth enjoyed the joke, Rose and Oliver contemplated this new dead end.

"There are no more stories about Patria in the *Chronicles?*" she asked.

"This is the last volume," Oliver replied.

"So we're out of clues to the whereabouts of the Treaty," sighed Farnsworth.

"Probably," said Oliver. "But if you're game, I have one more idea."

"So it's you boys again," yawned the Storyteller as he emerged from the bark hut that served as the tribe's guest quarters. "Not only do you destroy performances, you destroy *naps* as well. And who is this girl? Is she a drama-hater, too?"

Farnsworth introduced Rose to the Storyteller and then said; "We're very sorry, sir. We wouldn't have disturbed you if lives didn't depend upon it."

"*Lives?*" smirked the Storyteller.

Farnsworth turned to Oliver and with his eyes urged him to continue. Oliver took a deep breath. He didn't know how he was going to say what he needed to say without making the Storyteller angry. But he had to try.

"Last night, sir," he began, "Chief Albert asked if you knew any stories about Turkey Beard—"

The Storyteller's jaw muscles hardened and his

eyes narrowed as they studied Oliver.

"We were hoping that you would know something about what happened on the day the Treaty was signed between Patria and the United States."

The Storyteller looked over their heads and surveyed the camp, as if to make sure that no one was overhearing them. Then he said with a sneer:

"Did you not understand the answer I gave Chief Albert?"

"I did," said Oliver. "But you didn't actually tell him that you *didn't* know any stories about Turkey Beard."

Oliver closed his eyes, expecting the full force of the Storyteller's fury. Instead, he heard the Storyteller say in a stern voice—

"Come inside."

A deerskin rug covered one end of the guest quarters, and on it were spread large, comfy pillows with beaded designs. The only light in the house came from the hole directly in the center of the roof, out of which escaped the smoke from the fire when it was lit.

"Please, have a seat," said the Storyteller, motioning with irritation at the pillows on the deerskin rug. After Oliver, Farnsworth and Rose were settled on the pillows, he looked down at them and said solemnly:

"Not every story I know is a story I am free to tell."

"Do you mean we have to be Potawatomi to hear stories about Turkey Beard?" asked Farnsworth.

The Storyteller shook his head.

"Not every story I know is a story even Potawatomi may hear."

"But this is important," said Farnsworth. "As I said, lives may depend upon it."

Rose quickly ran through the basics of the conflict between Patria and Mr. Stoop.

"I'm afraid, sir," said Oliver when Rose had finished, "that without the Treaty, we don't stand any chance of keeping the two sides from fighting."

The Storyteller sat down upon a pillow and closed his eyes. He sat for a long time without speaking, breathing gently as he meditated upon the problem.

When he finally opened his eyes he said:

"I do not know how this will help you find the Treaty—but I will tell you what I know. When I was a young man, still learning the art that has made me the most distinguished Storyteller in the world, an aged Potawatomi Storyteller came to my village. Among the many stories he told me during his visit was one about Turkey Beard. *However*, this visiting Storyteller warned me that I was never to tell the story to anyone but a fellow storyteller. The story comes from the mouth of Turkey Beard himself, and has been kept alive by Potawatomi storytellers for many generations, so that the memory would not be lost. But the story has never—I repeat, *never*—been told outside of the company of storytellers."

The Storyteller examined each of them carefully.

"Until now. Today, I will tell you this story, but only because I believe Turkey Beard himself would have wanted me to do so. He would not have wanted Patria to suffer in such a useless war, especially if he could have helped to prevent it."

And so the Storyteller began:

"As all Patrians know from their *Patriad*, the Treaty of Alliance between Patria and the United States of America was signed on October 20, 1808. So much is true. But it is also said in the *Patriad* that, directly after the Treaty was signed, the party gathered at the Council Oak was attacked by a band of Americans, supposedly angry with Patria for daring to establish a kingdom inside their country. Afterwards, Sir Mycroft Malchio, Knight of the Blue Sock, captured and accused my Potawatomi brother Turkey Beard of helping plot the attack—and also for murdering his dear friend, Odysseus Murgatroyd.

"This much is *not* true.

"What really happened is this. In the raid at the Council Oak, Turkey Beard gave chase to one of the barbarians—a fact that was later used to accuse Turkey Beard of disappearing during the raid. He followed the raider to the castle. As Turkey Beard searched the castle for the rapscallion, he came down the corridor to the castle library. It was there he heard the sound of a scuffle, then a cry from his friend, Odysseus. Turkey Beard ran, and when he came to the library entrance he found Odysseus lying gravely wounded on the library floor. And standing over him with the bloodied knife—*Sir Mycroft Malchio!*

"Turkey Beard started for the murderer, but he didn't notice one of Malchio's treacherous henchmen, the very one he had been pursuing, sneaking up on him from behind. He was captured, and Malchio ordered him thrown into the castle dungeons. Turkey Beard had already been taken away by the time King Priam entered the library and found his friend Odysseus near death. Sir Mycroft Malchio blamed the murder on Turkey Beard, and King Priam, who thought of Malchio as a most faithful Blue Sock, believed him. The rest of what is written in the *Patriad* about Odysseus Murgatroyd's final moments is true."

After several silent moments Farnsworth said. "I don't believe it. Sir Mycroft Malchio was one of the greatest Blue Socks there ever was!"

"The story comes from Turkey Beard himself,"

replied the Storyteller coldly.

"Why would Sir Mycroft want to betray Patria?" demanded Rose.

"Sir Mycroft did not want peace with the Americans," replied the Storyteller. "He wanted to drive Americans out of this region, expand Patria's territory, turn your kingdom into an empire."

"Then why were the raiders Americans?" demanded Farnsworth.

"A bunch of n'er-do-wells," said the Storyteller, "handsomely paid by Sir Mycroft to stir up mischief at the Council Oak."

"This is ridiculous," Farnsworth snorted. "It goes against everything in the *Patriad*."

"Everything in the *Patriad* about this incident is taken from the account provided by *Sir Mycroft*," snorted the Storyteller in return.

"Somebody lied," concluded Rose, "either Sir Mycroft or Turkey Beard."

Oliver had been sitting quietly listening to this sharp exchange.

"Excuse me," he said. "I don't understand—why didn't Turkey Beard write in the *Chronicles* about what he saw?"

"You are perfectly correct to notice," said the Storyteller, turning to Oliver, "that Turkey Beard wrote no account of these events in the *Chronicles*. This was at the request of President Thomas

Jefferson himself. You see, it did not take Turkey Beard long to escape from the castle dungeons. Knowing that his life was in danger in Patria, he rode swiftly to Washington, D.C., where he explained to President Jefferson all that had happened. By that time, Jefferson had received from his messenger the United States copy of the Treaty of Alliance. He sent troops to Patria, to demand the handing over of the murderer of his ambassador. But by the time the troops arrived in Patria, they found—"

"—that Sir Mycroft Malchio had been killed," finished Rose. She turned to Oliver and explained: "Several days after Turkey Beard escaped, Sir Mycroft was murdered by some of the raiders still lurking in the Wyvern Weald. It's all at the end of the *Patriad*, Part 14."

The Storyteller added: "But the *Patriad* makes of it a hero's death. What really happened is that Sir Mycroft, because his band of n'er-do-wells failed to destroy all copies of the Treaty, refused to pay them what he promised. They didn't take it, shall we say, kindly."

"But what about Turkey Beard?" insisted Oliver. "I still don't understand why he didn't write about all this in the *Chronicles*."

"President Jefferson begged Turkey Beard to publish no more stories about Patria," resumed the Storyteller. "Although Sir Mycroft's scheme had been exposed, he was afraid that if word of Patria's existence spread abroad, those who did not like the idea of sharing this great land with a tiny kingdom would seek to harm it. Turkey Beard honored the president's wish. Indeed, he honored it so well that he didn't even tell his story generally to his own tribe, who for over two hundred years have believed him to be a traitor."

"So what do you think now, Farnsworth?" Rose asked her brother as the three of them walked back to the castle. "Do you think Sir Mycroft Malchio was a traitor to Patria?"

"I don't know," replied Farnsworth glumly.

"The Storyteller was right about one thing," Oliver said. "None of this brings us one step closer to finding the missing Treaty."

CHAPTER THIRTEEN

THE CEASE-FIRE CEASES

O liver couldn't sleep that night. There was just too much on his mind. Finally, he gave up trying and lit the candle on his bedside table. He picked up the last volume of the *Chronicles* from where he had hidden the book underneath his pillow and began to re-read the stories about Patria in light of what the Storyteller had told them that afternoon about Turkey Beard. He had been reading for about fifteen minutes when he heard a sound most unusual for the Kingdom of Patria.

Oliver knew instantly that there was only one machine in the world with a two-stroke diesel engine capable of such a contented purr.

He jumped into his clothes and—grabbing the *Chronicles*—dashed down the main staircase of the castle. Following the sound of the Lawn Beast, he took the moat bridge at the back of the castle. As he came pounding down its boards, he saw the Lawn Beast, its headlights on, gliding along the greensward as if coming from the Royal Stables.

At the wheel of the Beast was his father, and balanced on one of the running boards was Bill in her buckskin outfit, musket in hand!

"STOP STOOP!"

It was Sir Hector, in his nightshirt and flashing his sword as he followed Oliver down the moat bridge as fast as his creaky joints could carry him.

Mr. Stoop spied Oliver and tooted the Lawn Beast's horn.

"Get on, Oliver!" he yelled as he hit the brake. "I told you these nutcrackers stole my lawn mower!"

"What is that devilish mechanism, Stoop?" cried Sir Hector, who seemed more afraid of what might come out of the Lawn Beast than out of Bill's musket.

"As if you didn't know, you old prune!" Mr. Stoop shouted back. "You thought you could pull one over on Reginald Stoop."

"This is supposed to be a cease-fire, Stoop!" roared Sir Hector. "And yet you have come and attacked us, in the middle of the night no less, on that infernal iron horse! The cease-fire is over. Do you hear me?"

Sir Hector raised his sword and bellowed:

"WE...ARE...NOW...AT...WAR!"

Hearing that, Bill happily pinged a shot off of the tip of Sir Hector's sword. Sir Hector, not entirely clear whether or not Bill was a lady, decided that, with bullets flying, this was not the moment to explore the question. He hopped onto the greensward and to the safety of a nearby elm.

"GET ON, OLIVER!" shouted Mr. Stoop. "I'M GETTING YOU OUT OF HERE."

Oliver looked up at the castle—he wondered if the candlelight he saw in one of the windows was from Farnsworth's room. He didn't want to leave them, *not now…*

"NOW, OLIVER!"

He had no choice. He climbed up on the running board of the Lawn Beast opposite Bill.

"Come sunrise, Stoop," shouted Sir Hector, poking his head out from behind the elm, "you will feel the full force of the famed Knights of the Blue Sock!"

"Don't forget to bring your little toy swords!" laughed Mr. Stoop as he slid the Lawn Beast into gear.

"YAWR-HOO!" crowed Bill, and fired a gleeful shot into the air.

And so, with the Lawn Beast in fifth gear, Oliver, Mr. Stoop, and Bill zipped home through the Wyvern Weald.

Mr. Stoop's thoughts were all bent on war. He said to Oliver: "Me and the Midwest War-Historicals will handle this situation ourselves. Though I've given us a new name: the *Stoop Freedom Fighters.* It's going to be like the Old West, Oliver, when men protected their families with six-shooters!"

Bill crowed and fired another round into the night.

But Oliver wasn't happy about the prospect of a battle. He was thinking about how much he already missed them: Farnsworth and Princess Rose, Professor Vesuvius and Lady Lavinia—even Sasquatch. Strange, he had hardly gotten to know them, but already he counted them, especially Farnsworth and Rose, as the best friends he ever had.

While Mr. Stoop secured the Lawn Beast with the new security system he had bought for the utility shed, Bill returned to the truck where Pete was asleep behind the wheel and spread out her sleeping bag in the bed.

Oliver looked back across the Cow Park to the Wyvern Weald. How strange it was to think that this was the same woods of which, two days before, he had been so afraid. Now, that wall of trees struck him like the front curtain at a theater, behind which waited a miraculous and marvelous world.

But would he ever see his friends in Patria again?

Had the quest come to its end? Was there really going to be a war?

Oliver dragged himself up the front stairs and into the mobile home.

As he set up his tent again, he listened to his parents arguing behind their closed door.

"...they're not going to *attack* us, Reginald."

"They just declared war on us! *War*, Phoebe. If those lunatics so much as place *one foot* upon my property—"

"What Reginald? What are you going to do? Chase after them with the lawn mower? Maybe you can perform the "French & Indian Wars" sketch for them."

"Go ahead and laugh! I already have Pete rounding up the team. They'll be here bright and early in the morning, waiting for those wackos. If they come onto my land, it'll be no re-enactment, let me tell you!"

"I wish you men would just leave everything to me and Lady Lavinia," lamented Mrs. Stoop. "None of this nonsense would ever have started, and that sweet Sir Amory would be going out with Hazel."

"They just about deserve each other," chortled Mr. Stoop.

His tent back up, Oliver found a fresh pair of pajamas and nestled into his sleeping bag. He still had the *Chronicles* with him, and turning on his flashlight he, for the second time that night, settled in with it. He glanced again at the two stories Turkey Beard had written about Patria, and then turned to the story he had been reading when he was mowing the Cow Park with the Lawn Beast, the day he had met Farnsworth and Rose and Flying Squirrel.

It was called, remember, "Irritations Among the Iroquois." Oliver was at that point in the story when Odysseus Murgatroyd and Turkey Beard are paddling downriver and find themselves being followed by a band of Iroquois warriors, angry at Turkey Beard for proposing marriage to their princess. While the Iroquois canoe was still far away, Odysseus Murgatroyd ordered Turkey Beard to hide under a pile of beaver pelts…

And when the Iroquois canoe came even with ours, one of the Iroquois warriors addressed Odysseus:

"Have you seen a Potawatomi scout who thinks him good enough to marry Iroquois princess?" The warrior didn't really expect the white man to understand him, yet Odysseus replied in flawless Iroquois:

"He's quite nearby. I last saw him in a canoe."

The Iroquois' eyebrows jerked upward.

"Thanks much, honorable white man."

And he and his band, assuming—falsely—that Odysseus meant that he had seen me pass him in my own canoe, paddled on.

"Fast thinking," I said to Odysseus, lifting a pelt from my face and smiling with admiration at my old friend.

"It is beneath me to lie, Turkey Beard, even to a band of Iroquois warriors seeking a scalp," said Odysseus complacently. "It is perfectly true that you are quite nearby, and that I last saw you in a canoe."

Oliver stopped, his mouth slightly ajar, his mind whirring. Odysseus Murgatroyd was always so clever with words....

Putting his finger in the page, Oliver flipped forward to the story he had read aloud to Farnsworth and Rose at lunch:

Odysseus and King Priam quickly became good friends, as they shared a love of clever wordplay. Their conversation was littered with all manner of puns and riddles....

Then Oliver recalled the passages from the *Patriad* he had read the night before in the castle. During the raid, Odysseus Murgatroyd had taken Patria's copy of the Treaty back to the castle to hide it. So why hadn't he told King Priam the hiding place?

With the very last breath that Odysseus mustered
He uttered the words of a deep mystery:
said to King Priam as his soul took its leaving:
"You will always, my friend, find an ally in me."

Of course! Odysseus Murgatroyd didn't want to reveal the hiding place of the Treaty, because along with King Priam, *Sir Mycroft Malchio was kneeling right there beside him.*

Oliver shot out of the sleeping bag as though a scorpion waiting at the bottom had just unleashed its stinger on his foot. He tore off his pajamas and began to dress.

He had to get back to the castle—*tonight!*

Chapter Fourteen
Belly of the Beast

O liver heard them singing as he scooted across the greensward to a hiding place in the summerhouse. It was nearly dawn, but the Knights of the Blue Sock were up and armored, and they sang as they mounted their horses up by the moat.

Better use the privvy, Sir Henry!
Better use the privvy, Sir Ray!
Cause when you're locked into your armor
And nature sounds the alarmer
You'll wait upon relief all daaaaay!

Each knight wore the colors of his clan, and they made a brilliant mix of stripes, hoops and diamonds; hearts, squares and zigzags; solids and tartans in every conceivable color. The horses, too, were decked out in the colors of their masters' clans, all the way down to their masks and plumes. Along the line, one could hear loud snorts and impatient grunts—though which were from the horses and which were from Sir Hector was not always clear.

From the doorway of the summerhouse Oliver watched breathlessly as Sir Hector rode in front of the line to address the troops.

"Noble Blue Socks! Today, for the first time since the Almost Civil War with the Geats of 1932, our company has assembled in arms. This is the *decisive* battle of our age. Our *entire lives* have been but a preparation for this moment. A usurping Stoop has seized the Cow Park. He has assembled an army. He has broken a cease-fire. He has attacked us with an iron horse spitting fire straight out of Hell!"

The Blue Socks roared their anger and shook their swords.

"But we will not allow this savage Stoop to take our land! We are men of Patria! We are Blue Socks! I say BLUE!"

"WE SAY SOCKS!" sang the Blue Socks heartily.

"Would you like to say a word, King Evander?" said Sir Hector to his brother. The king, sitting on his horse behind the line of Blue Socks, was busy jotting down in his notebook possible rhymes for *usurper*. So far, he had only come up with: *You burper*.

"EVANDER!" thundered Sir Hector. "Say something to inspire the troops!"

"Eh?" said the king. "Say something? Quite

right. I will say something. I say it's dashed difficult to find a place for one's notebook in all this armor. No pockets."

"HUZZAH!" shouted the knights.

The Blue Socks were soon joined by a hearty band of Geat warriors, along with a number of Geat wives who would not be kept at home, as well as by a company of Potawatomi warriors, headed by Chief Albert. As soon as the entire Patrian army was assembled, Sir Hector and King Evander led them up the rolling greensward toward the Wyvern Weald as the sun crept up behind the trees.

Patria! O Patria!
The greatest land not on the maps!
Though our knee-joints be rusty,
Our hearts will be trusty,
As soon as we're up from our naps!

Oliver crouched low in the summerhouse and waited for them to pass. He didn't have much time. Even if his crazy idea turned out to be right, he still had to sneak down into the castle, find the Treaty, and get back to the Cow Park before the fighting began.

But first, he had to wake up Farnsworth.

"WHACHYAWACKADOODLE!"

Farnsworth, shall we say, was a little surprised when Oliver shook him awake.

"Oliver! What are you doing here? Did I miss the battle?"

"Get the Studebaker," whispered Oliver. "Be waiting for me in front of the castle."

"Why? What's going on?"

"No time to explain."

"Got it," Farnsworth nodded, and he was halfway into his clothes before Oliver even left the room.

Oliver scurried through the castle to the library, breathlessly repeating to himself: *Don't think. Just go in and do it.*

He entered the library, where the rising sun was splashing golden light through the tall windows. He ran straight to the standing wax figure of Odysseus Murgatroyd. This was the only plan he had, and he prayed that it would work.

He began to look for some opening, some hiding place in the wax that the heroic woodsman would have used to hide the Treaty. He didn't have much time. Then again, neither had Odysseus Murgatroyd.

Which gave Oliver an idea.

He grabbed a short ladder left at a nearby bookshelf, and climbing halfway up it he was able to lift the genuine coonskin cap off the head of the wax figure, as well as the golden wig underneath. Oliver then saw, on the bald head of Odysseus Murgatroyd's wax figure, a round plug of wax, like the rubber stopper on his old piggy bank. Odysseus, Oliver guessed, had cut out a hole into the wax with his bear knife, stuffed the Treaty down the hollow insides of his own figure, and then used the wax he had cut out for a plug. Under the wig and the coonskin cap, the wax plug had remained a secret for over two hundred years.

"You will always, my friend, find an ally in me."

In me. The woodsman who excelled in clever wordplay had tried to communicate to King Priam the Treaty's hiding place by way of a *riddle*—so as not to reveal the hiding place to the wicked Sir Mycroft. Oliver dug out the wax plug with his fingers. He then reached down into the hole, and— there it was! A scroll of parchment that could only be the Treaty of Alliance between Patria and the United States of America!

In the two centuries that had passed since Odysseus Murgatroyd had hid the Treaty in his wax figure, the parchment had become dry and brittle, and Oliver was very careful as he lifted it out of its hiding place.

"Master Oliver. What a pleasure to see you again."

"AWAH-HA!" cried Oliver as he whipped around, his body rattling. He found Miching Malchio strolling across the library towards him, with Sasquatch on one side of him and the man with stringy, greasy hair whom he had seen at Bubbles & Burps.

At first Oliver was relieved to see that it was only King Evander's private secretary. But when he saw the man with stringy, greasy hair, he realized he was in danger. He and Malchio were smiling at Oliver with menacing smiles, and it was those awful smiles more than anything else that convinced Oliver that these two men, in ridiculous disguise, had been the Mr. Blaggard and Mr. Squilch who had sold Mr. Stoop the Cow Park.

"You must understand, Master Oliver," said Malchio, "that now that Patria has declared war against the Republic of Staplers, we are going to have to arrest you."

Oliver quickly stuffed the scroll down his shirt.

"What is that, boy?" inquired Malchio. But Oliver saw in Malchio's eyes that he had already guessed what it was.

"Sasquatch! Dogsbody! Seize him!"

Dogsbody? So this was also the man whom Rose had seen reading the last volume of the *Chronicles* in Oliver's room.

"Forgeeve me, Master Olywer," said Sasquatch, looking as though he would much rather have been serving Oliver his morning rasher of bacon than arresting him. "It being my duty."

"Of c-c-course, Sasquatch," replied Oliver. "I p-p-perfectly understand. Hope you don't mind if I make a run for it?"

Sasquatch shrugged his mountainous shoulders. "It only sporting."

Oliver ran. With his pursuers between him and the entrance to the library, the only thing was to run toward the bookshelves on the other side of the Trojan Tub.

With huge, hulking strides Sasquatch pounded after him, Dogsbody looking happy to let the beast of a butler take the lead.

A plan starting to form in his mind, Oliver began to climb one of the rolling ladders that Professor Vesuvius used to reach books and scrolls on the higher shelves. Being not just fearful, but absolutely petrified of anything higher than a bunk bed, Oliver climbed with his eyes closed. He just kept reaching for the next rung and stepping up.

Sasquatch's hand closed upon his shoe. Oliver kicked himself free, and began pulling rows of old books off the shelves and raining them down upon the poor butler. After plunking Sasquatch on the head with *The Lost Dialogues of Aristotle,* Oliver had the space he needed to get to the top of the ladder—where one of Professor Vesuvius' gliding chairs awaited him.

Now came the hard part. He threw a last couple of tomes at Sasquatch, and then one or two at the disgusting Dogsbody, who took the thick, weighty *Burial Customs of the Estruscans* square in the face and collapsed.

This was it. There was no turning back.

Holding onto a bookshelf, Oliver jumped into the chair. Then, remembering how Professor Vesuvius had done it, he flipped the latch and pushed himself away from the bookshelf—

ZZZZZiiiiiiiiiiiiiiiiiinnnnnGGGGG!

The angle and thickness of the cable ensured that the chair did not travel too speedily. As he passed over the Trojan Tub's figurehead, he had plenty of time to hook his foot on the carved horse's mane and stop himself.

The back of the horse's head was almost as wide as a stair, and the very top of the head, just as flat as one. Sliding forward in the chair, Oliver reached down and was able to place his foot on the head of the horse. Hanging onto the chair for balance, he slid forward and placed his other foot down.

Then slowly, one finger at a time, Oliver let go off the chair, until he was standing, unassisted, on the top of the figurehead of the Trojan Tub!

"Get him, Sasquatch!" shouted Malchio.

Oliver felt a tug on the cable. Sasquatch had jumped off the ladder and was looping toward him with jumbo swings.

In a single movement, Oliver swung his body underneath the snout of the horse and dropped into the wooden animal's wide-open mouth.

He slid fast down the horse's throat, like the slide at school when kids threw sand on it, and landed hard in the hollow belly of the beast. He scrambled to his feet and started shoving against the sides of the vessel. It took three shoves before he found the door. He leapt down to the ground, just as Malchio was coming around to grab him. But Oliver gave the king's private secretary the old football stiff-arm right in the face, and Malchio collapsed like a marionette, holding his nose.

"SBY!" Oliver heard Malchio screech behind him. "SBY IN THE CASTLE OF PATRIA!"

CHAPTER FIFTEEN

THE HISTORIC, MOMENTOUS BATTLE OF THE COW PARK

With Slobberchops bouncing at his side, Farnsworth had the Studebaker chugging and spitting on the greensward as Oliver flew out of the castle. He told Oliver to take the wheel, so that he could sit on his knees facing backwards and hold off pursuers with the Magna-Pneumatic.

"Hoo-boy! This is fun," squawked Farnsworth. "Where we going?"

"The Cow Park," said Oliver. Farnsworth hooted even louder and grabbed three more whizzing biscuits from the bag slung over his shoulder and dropped them down the pipe of his weapon.

Oliver stamped on the gas pedal and they were off.

"I've got the Treaty," he shouted over the rumble of the old car as it bumped over the greensward toward the Wyvern Weald.

"*What?*" gasped Farnsworth. "How did you—? I mean, *where* did you—?"

"No time," Oliver hollered. "We've got to get to the Cow Park and stop the battle before Malchio catches us."

"*Malchio?*" erupted Farnsworth.

They hadn't made it to the edge of the Weald before Farnsworth spotted someone on a horse bearing down upon them from the castle.

"Oh, good grief!"

"Who is it?" cried Oliver. "Malchio? Or Sasquatch?"

"*My sister!*"

Oliver looked over his shoulder to see, and there was Princess Rose galloping over the greensward. The Studebaker was no match for Hecuba, so Rose caught up with them well before they made the Weald. As she got close, she reached back behind her and yanked a sword out of a scabbard slung across her back. She rode alongside the Studebaker and, in a nimble maneuver, used her sword to prong two biscuits out of Farnsworth's bag. Letting go of the reins, she grabbed the first biscuit with her free hand, and plunked her brother on the head with it.

"That's for leaving me behind!" she said.

Then she plunked him on the head with the second one.

"And that's for using my biscuits for ammunition!"

Farnsworth grabbed his head. Whizzing biscuits, he discovered, really hurt—especially when thrown from extremely close range.

"You should have come and got me," said Rose rather sternly to Oliver as she picked up her horse's reins again.

Oliver grimaced his apology, actually quite happy to escape with no more than a firm rebuke.

"Look!" shouted Farnsworth. "Here comes Malchio!"

A horseman was in hot pursuit of them across the greensward. The inky figure in the saddle clearly identified him as Miching Malchio.

"What's he doing?" asked Rose.

Oliver replied: "He thinks I'm a spy and that I'm stealing the Treaty." He flattened the gas pedal. "Can't this thing go any faster?"

"Malchio's not alone," Farnsworth shouted. "Here comes Sasquatch on foot. WHA-HOOO! Isn't this fun?"

The Studebaker charged into the Weald, with Malchio and Sasquatch gaining on them by the second.

"They're going to catch us!" cried Oliver.

"Not to worry," replied Farnsworth, loading the Magna-Pneumatic with a whizzing biscuit.

"Let me help!" shouted Rose.

She pulled up on Hecuba's reins and turned

round and charged their pursuers. From behind him Oliver heard Malchio's squealing voice.

"Princess! I'm here to *defend* you. That boy has stolen the Treaty of—*ahhhhh!*"

Malchio had not been able to finish his thought. Oliver turned and saw that it was everything Malchio could do to duck the slash of Rose's sword as she galloped past him toward Sasquatch.

But quickly recovering from Rose's attack, Malchio closed upon the Studebaker.

"Stop the car, Prince Farnsworth," Malchio shouted. "That boy is stealing the Treaty of Alliance."

"And I'm helping him," Farnsworth called back as he popped a whizzing biscuit into the carriage of the Magna-Pneumatic. He aimed at Malchio's beaky nose and, with a yip of encouragement from Slobberchops, fired.

"Did you get him?" asked Oliver.

"Got his horse," answered Farnsworth.

Oliver looked over his shoulder. Malchio's horse had reeled, but Sasquatch was bearing down on them—with Rose right at his side:

"Sasquatch!" she snapped at him, thumping him on the head with her sword. "Shame on you. You know Master Oliver is only trying to help Patria."

"Billion apologies, Your Highness. Only doing duty."

"Your duty is to defend the Royal Family of Patria!

As Rose continued to thump the gargantuan butler on the head with her sword, Farnsworth kept firing. He bunged another biscuit into the Magna-Pneumatic, aimed in the general direction of Malchio's head, and fired. The biscuit clunked Malchio right in the ear. His body jerked sideways, just as the horse, reaching a turn in the path, swung in the opposite direction. In this clash of opposing forces Malchio lost his balance and fell. He toppled into some bramble at the side of the path as Farnsworth, shaking the Magna-Pneumatic above his head, proclaimed *"Vic-tor-eeeeee!"*

Minutes later, the Studebaker crashed through the last wall of bramble into the Cow Park. The Knights of the Blue Sock were lined up on horseback along the edge of the field, with Sir Hector positioned in the middle of the line, next to King Evander, so that a wing of knights formed on both their left and their right.

Behind the knights, also on horseback, were the Geat warriors and most of their wives. The Potawatomi had taken up positions in the trees and in the shrubs.

Mr. Stoop and the Stoop Freedom Fighters

were more or less assembled in front of the Stoop mobile home. In the middle of the line facing the Patrian army, Mr. Stoop had taken his place astride the Lawn Beast, whose turbo-charged, two-stroke diesel engine barely disturbed the solemn hush of the June morning.

After Farnsworth helped him stop the car, Oliver ran up to where his father had gathered with his War Council.

"Oliver, where have you been? Where did you get that old Studie?"

"Dad, I need to talk—" Oliver huffed.

"Oliver, *get inside*. There's no telling what those maniacs across the way might do."

"Dad—"

"They got some *sweet* uniforms, eh chief?" Pete said to Mr. Stoop. "What battle is it exactly they re-enactin'?"

"This is the battle for my little slice of the American Dream," declared Mr. Stoop, a dramatic finger raised to the heavens. "And it's *no* re-enactment."

"Whatchoo mean no re-enactment, chief?" said Pete, looking anxious.

"Reginald! What are you doing? Stop this *right now!"*

Mrs. Stoop, still in her bathrobe and holding a half-eaten microwaveable breakfast burrito, had appeared in the doorway of the mobile home with Aunt Hazel peering curiously over her shoulder.

Sir Amory's sigh could be heard across the field.

"Don't worry, sweetie," Mr. Stoop said, patting his rifle affectionately. "This will all be over in a moment."

"You're not going to *shoot* at those people, Reginald! Do you hear me?"

Pete interjected, as delicately as he could, that his wife probably wouldn't like him spending his Saturday morning shooting at people for real.

"I haven't the slightest intention of shooting anyone," said Mr. Stoop calmly. "I'm simply going to fire a round or two in the air, and that bunch of rodeo clowns will gallop hysterically back into the woods. They still fight with *swords!*"

"Reginald! Put down that gun *this instant.*"

A trumpet sounded from the Patrian side—followed by a medley of hacking and coughing from the trumpeter.

Figuring that this meant that the Patrian army was getting ready to charge, Oliver, joined by Farnsworth and Slobberchops, beat it to the Patrian side of the field.

"YAWR-HOO!" whooped Bill from her crouching position in the bed of Pete's truck. "Some fun!"

As Oliver and Farnsworth approached the Patrian line, Oliver heard Sir Hector barking orders to Sir Amory, who was surveying the field with a spyglass.

"Assessment, Sir Amory?"

"Well, Sir Hector, she looks rather tired this morning, as though she hasn't slept well. Poor darling. This war has wreaked havoc on her nerves."

"BLAST IT, AMORY! I'm not talking about the Witch Hazel. I'm talking about the Stoop Army!"

Startled, Sir Amory turned the spyglass away from the mobile home and made a quick survey of the battlefield.

"King Evander," quivered Oliver, looking up at the distracted monarch, who at the moment was trying to think of an appropriate rhyme for "Stoop." "I need to talk with you."

"Away, boy!" bellowed Sir Hector. "Leave it to Stoop to put his son in the path of a conquering army."

"I see Stoop," reported Sir Amory. "He has a rifle. Are we using rifles, Sir Hector?"

The waxed tips of Sir Hector's moustache quivered.

"The only way to fight fire, Sir Amory, is with fire."

"There she is!" cried Sir Amory, whose spyglass

had wandered back to the doorway of the mobile home. "I think she's looking for me, Hector." Sir Amory waved. "Don't worry, my darling! If I die today, it will be for you!"

"BLUE SOCKS!" Sir Hector boomed. "PREPARE FOR BATTLE!"

"I'm not sure what I'm supposed to *do*, Hector," whined one of the knights.

"Just follow my lead, Sir Fergal. And Evander, put down that notebook. Its customary for poets to write their war tales *after the fighting is over.*"

"Just taking some notes, Hector," said the king. "Now how would you describe the color of Mrs. Stoop's bathrobe? Mauve? Or would you simply call it purple?"

"King Evander, *please!*" tried Oliver one more time. But Sir Hector ordered one of the Geats to take Oliver aside.

"ARMS AT THE READY!" shouted Sir Hector. He reached back over his shoulder to where his rifle was strapped against his back. He gripped the rifle by its neck and pulled. With a neat twirl over his head, he brought the rifle down in front of him, so that Mr. Stoop's forehead appeared squarely in the center of the sighting.

The remaining knights were not quite so successful with the maneuver.

"Arrrgggh! I think I pulled something in my

shoulder."

"My word, Hector, you must be double-jointed."

"Great frozen gherkins! I forgot my gun."

In the arms of the burly Geat warrior Oliver looked on with horror as the Blue Socks and Potawatomi readied their guns. The Geats, it seemed, even in this modern era, preferred hatchets, daggers, and broadswords.

On the other side of the field, the Stoop Freedom Fighters took up the positions assigned to them in the "Battle of Fort Wayne" sketch.

Sir Hector shouted: "READY…AIM…"

But before he shouted "FIRE!" there was a shot.

A *real* shot.

From a *real* gun.

A shot that shattered the golden morning.

A shot that ended centuries of peace.

A single shot, Oliver saw when he opened his eyes, that—miraculously—took down *nine* Knights of the Blue Sock and *almost all* the members of the Stoop Freedom Fighters.

The Historic, Momentous Battle of the Cow Park had begun.

CHAPTER SIXTEEN

GOLDEN EAGLE HAS LANDED

How was it possible? *A single bullet striking down all these men?* It was against all the laws of physics.

Oliver was relieved to find his father still sitting on the Lawn Beast, looking with disbelief at his fallen comrades. Then, to his amazement, Oliver saw Pete lift his head from the ground to see if the shooting was over.

Oliver whirled around. Several of the fallen knights were also stirring.

"I didn't shoot!" howled Mr. Stoop. *"It wasn't me!"*

"It wasn't us!" thundered Sir Hector in reply. *"I didn't give the order to fire. The shot came from your end, Stoop!"*

From the bed of Pete's truck came the sound of creaky laughter as Bill prepared to drop another lead ball down the shaft of her musket.

"Bill!" shouted Pete at his mother-in-law. *"No more shootin'! You hear me? You're gonna get us all*

killed!"

Bill quizzed her son-in-law with her better eye.

"Is this a battle, boy, or a Sunday school picnic?"

Thus the Historic, Momentous Battle of the Cow Park had started with a zealous shot by Bill. The wiry old woman, intending to put a scare into the enemy, had aimed a good six inches above the head of Sir Hector and ripped the bark off an oak tree twenty yards behind him.

"Stop!" shouted Oliver as he struggled free of the Geat warrior and ran out into the field. *"No more shooting! You must stop! I have the Treaty—I have the Treaty right here!"*

Oliver reached inside his shirt and handed to King Evander the scroll of parchment.

King Evander took the scroll and carefully began to open it. But before he could begin to read, he was interrupted by a shriek of panic.

"DON'T READ THAT, YOUR MAJESTY!"

The shriek came from Miching Malchio, who along with Sasquatch was being led into the Cow Park at the point of Rose's sword.

"Malchio!" cried King Evander. "This is no time for dictation!"

"Your Majesty," panted Malchio, "if I may beg your pardon. What you hold in your hand is a forgery."

"What? What are you talking about, Malchio?"

"A trick, Your Highness, played by this spawn of Stoop. The boy snuck back into the castle early this morning to make it look like he had discovered the whereabouts of the original Treaty of Alliance."

"That's not true!" protested Oliver boldly. "I *did* find the real Treaty."

"Your Majesty," Malchio continued, "the forgery in your hand no doubt claims that the Cow Park belongs to the United States of America."

"Eh?" said King Evander. "It does? I couldn't say. I haven't read that far."

"Allow me to save you the trouble, Your Majesty. Of course it claims that the Cow Park rightfully belongs to the United States, which would mean that now, by just exchange, it belongs to the President of the Republic of Staplers. What else would it say? We all know the Stoops will stop at nothing to get their hands on the Cow Park. Fortunately, we have the means at our disposal of exposing this charade."

"We do?" said the king.

"We do," said Malchio. And out of the inside pocket of his coat he produced a piece of folded parchment. He held it up high in the air for all to see.

"This, my friends, is the *real* Treaty of Alliance between Patria and the United States of America!"

Several of the knights who had dozed off while

lying on the ground awakened with the sound of Malchio's announcement.

"How did you find it, Malchio?" inquired Sir Hector.

"It was nothing," Malchio closed his eyes with a humble smile. "I was up late last night reading the memoirs of my revered ancestor, Sir Mycroft. Funny, I had never read the entire thing before. I turned a page, and there it was, neatly folded and tucked away—*the Treaty of Alliance*! Odysseus Murgatroyd must have given it to my ancestor to hide."

"Great blubbering catfish," said the king. "After all these years!"

"But what does the Treaty say about the Cow Park?" asked Sir Hector.

"Perhaps His Majesty would like to read it?" said Malchio as he brought the parchment to King Evander.

The king gave to Sir Hector the scroll that Oliver had given him and opened up Malchio's parchment.

"Ah!" mumbled the king.

"What does it say, Evander?" exploded Sir Hector.

"Well, there's a lot of chatter about our two great nations. Then there's a rather technical section about boundaries. Ah! Here we are. It says: *'And the entirety of the district, up to and including the field known by all as the Cow Park, shall hereafter belong—to*

Patria!'"

Huzzahs rang out among the Knights of the Blue Sock, Geats, and Potawatomi. Several began chanting, "MALCHIO FOR KING! MALCHIO FOR KING!" King Evander was louder than any of them.

Oliver pondered Malchio's dreamy expression as he bathed in this praise, and he understood all that Malchio had been up to. This seemingly loyal private secretary had been working fiendishly behind the scenes to *create* this war between Patria and Mr. Stoop, just so that, at the last minute, he could save the day with a fake Treaty—and get himself elected king. It was Malchio, with Dogsbody, who had sold the Cow Park to Mr. Stoop. Malchio who was behind the break-in at the mobile home and theft of the Lawn Beast. Just as it was no doubt Malchio who had ordered Dogsbody to search Oliver's suite for the last volume of the *Chronicles*.

Malchio's ancestor, Sir Mycroft, would have been proud.

"None of this is true!" shouted Oliver. "It's all a lie!"

"Hold your tongue, boy!" growled Sir Hector.

"I won't!" Oliver shot back, and he couldn't help notice the shocked expressions on the faces of Farnsworth and Rose. But he didn't care. He had to go on. He blurted out in one long breath, holding the Treaty in the air: "Odysseus Murgatroyd hid this Treaty in his own wax figure in the castle library. Sir Mycroft Malchio found him there and murdered him. It wasn't Turkey Beard. Sir Mycroft Malchio organized the whole attack at the Council Oak—he lied about everything!"

"Preposterous story" grunted Sir Hector. "Evander, announce to Stoop that we have finally found the Treaty of Alliance and that the Cow Park justly and finally belongs *to Patria*."

"You have GOT to be kidding me!" howled Mr. Stoop, who without anyone noticing had strolled up to the enemy line. "What do you lunatics take me for? I mean, how big of an idiot do you think I am? If you think I'm going to believe *that* paper is a Treaty signed by Thomas Jefferson, then you have seriously misjudged my mental capacities!"

"You have mental capacities?" inquired Sir Hector.

"Who's Thomas Jefferson?" asked the king.

Mr. Stoop began stomping up and down with both feet.

"GET OFF OF MY LAND, YOU BOZOS! GET OFF OF MY LAND OR THERE'S NO TELLING WHAT I'M GOING TO DO!"

And who knows what might have happened next if a loud, mechanical drone had not caused everyone to stop and look to the cloudless blue sky. Presently, over the line of oak trees, a black helicopter appeared.

"RE-TREEEEEEAT!" bellowed Sir Hector. "Into the woods! What is this awful new device, Stoop?"

But none of the knights was able to hear Sir Hector. Everyone had his hands over his ears.

Like a giant metal bee settling onto a flower, the helicopter hovered over a spot near the mobile before touching down. Immediately a door opened and out poured a whole platoon of United States Marines in full battle gear, toting machine guns. They fanned out across the field, barking at anyone with a weapon in his hand to drop it. With a wink, Bill handed her rifle to the Marine who had bounded up to her perch in the truck.

"WA-HOO!" cried Mr. Stoop. "Looky here, Oliver—it's the Marines! Hey guys! Arrest these loonies! They think they've got their own country on the other side of—"

Mr. Stoop did not have a chance to finish his thought. He was tackled by a Marine who grabbed the rifle out of his hand and pinned him to the ground.

"I can't tell you how glad I am to see you!" Mr. Stoop grinned at his captor.

When the Marines had secured the area, several men in dark suits emerged from the helicopter.

They approached King Evander, and Oliver heard one of them talking into the radio embedded in his ear.

"Field secure for Golden Eagle."

Everyone watched breathlessly as the hatch of the helicopter opened and several more dark-suited men in sunglasses hurried down the stairway. They formed two parallel lines and waited.

When the helicopter's propeller finally came to a complete rest, there was no other sound or movement in the entire field.

What appeared, finally, was nothing more threatening than a middle-aged man in a blue suit and red tie. He was still buttoning the jacket of his suit as he walked down the stairway.

At the sight of him, Oliver gasped.

Mr. Stoop exclaimed: "It's him! It's really him! He looks so much taller on television."

With the men in dark suits and sunglasses following closely at his side, the man in the blue suit strode across the field with grim determination. The Marines, machine guns at the ready, never took their eyes off either the Patrians or the Stoop Freedom Fighters.

"Which one of you is Mr. Stoop?" said the man as he approached.

Everyone pointed at the figure pinned upon the ground.

The man examined Mr. Stoop for a moment, and motioned for the Marine to help Mr. Stoop to his feet.

"Delighted, Mr. President," grinned Mr. Stoop, "to welcome you to our humble abode. I didn't vote for you, to be perfectly honest. But I hope you won't hold that against me."

"That's perfectly all right, Mr. Stoop," replied the president. "We live in a democracy."

"Are *you* the President of the United States?" asked King Evander.

"I am." And the President of the United States extended his hand to the king and introduced himself.

"It's an honor to meet you, sir. My name is Evander Jolly IV, King of Patria. This is my brother, Hector, Superior General of the Illustrious Order of Knights of the Blue Sock."

Captivated by the sight of the Patrian army, the president was not a little distracted as he shook hands.

"Mr. President," interjected Mr. Stoop, "although I didn't vote for you, I hope you will take my advice and keep your security guards close. None of these men you see before you are in their right mind—and don't even get me started on the women. They think they live in their own little kingdom called Patria, and that this field belongs to them and not to the United States."

"They do live in their own little kingdom called Patria," the president turned to Mr. Stoop.

"I beg your pardon?"

"Patria is a sovereign kingdom, Mr. Stoop, and has been recognized as such by the United States since the Jefferson administration."

It's hard to explain how these words, coming from the mouth of the President of the United States, affected Mr. Stoop. If the president had said that he was an alien being occupying a human body and that his species had come to take over Earth, Mr. Stoop would not have been more stunned.

"You mean…?"

"I was as surprised as you are, Mr. Stoop, when I found out about Patria."

"But—"

"I'm sure Thomas Jefferson was surprised, too, when he first learned of Odysseus Murgatroyd's discovery. But Jefferson was a great lover of freedom, and he respected the right of the Patrian people to exist. That's why he signed the Treaty of Alliance. Still, to protect Patria from any interference, he decided to keep it a secret from the American people. Jefferson designated Patria Area 1, a top-secret enclosure. In the early 19th century, keeping Patria hidden was a fairly easy thing to do. In the early 21st century, it's a whole lot more work keeping Patria from being discovered."

"Let 'em be discovered," said Mr. Stoop, "and thrown into the loony bin."

"It's not the Patrians' fault that our country has grown up around them," reflected the president. "They were here first, after all."

"I knew I was right not to vote for you," mumbled Mr. Stoop, and the hand of the Marine at his side clamped down upon his arm.

"So you know all about the Treaty with Sonny Jerkinstiff?" said King Evander.

"Thomas Jefferson," corrected the president. "And I do know all about the Treaty. The United States has a copy of the original Treaty in a secret vault in our National Archives, but I have a photocopy of it right here." He reached into the breast pocket of his suit jacket and pulled out a folded piece of paper.

He handed it to King Evander.

The king examined the photocopy of the Treaty that the president had given him, and compared it to the parchment that Malchio had given him.

"Great horned baboons!" he said.

"I beg your pardon?" said the president.

"Perhaps you can make sense of it," said the king as he handed the president the parchment that Malchio had given him. The president studied it in silence for several moments as Malchio looked on warily.

"Wow," said the president, "I'm holding a piece of paper with Thomas Jefferson's signature on it." The president shook his head in admiration. "Too bad it's a forgery."

King Evander was not a man whose mind was able to come to grips with the prospect of two forged treaties before lunch.

"I beg your pardon, sir?"

"This is a forgery. The Treaty between the United States and Patria does not claim that the Cow Park belongs to Patria."

"See there!" said Mr. Stoop, tearing his arm away from the grip of the Marine and doing a little dance that resembled an Irish jig performed by a giraffe. "Ha-ah! Take that, all you Patria people. The field is mine. *All mine.* I knew I would win in the end!"

"Hold on there, Mr. Stoop," said the president. "There's a bit more to the story."

Mr. Stoop froze in mid-jig.

"Where did you get this forgery?" the president asked King Evander.

King Evander and all the knights looked at Malchio—who, with a little devil-may-care laugh, said:

"I found it among the papers of this crazy ancestor of mine. Crazy Uncle Mycroft we call him. He's famous in our family for being a few pawns short of a chess set."

"Well, I think your ancestor was trying to pull a fast one," said the president. "I brought here today a photocopy of the Treaty delivered to President Jefferson, and it's significantly different from this one."

"Different? Really?" laughed Malchio. "Oh, that crazy Uncle Mycroft. It was probably part of some practical joke. Ah, well. You know what they say. You can't choose your relatives."

The president gauged Malchio carefully.

"So if that's the real Treaty in your hand," said Sir Hector to the president, "what does it say about the true ownership of the Cow Park?"

"I wish I could answer that, Sir Hector," said the president.

"What do you mean?" said King Evander. "Doesn't it say on the copy you brought from your Archives?"

The president took the photocopy back from King Evander.

"I wish it did," he said. "You may not know this, but in 1814 the United States was at war once again with Great Britain. On August 24th, the British burned down many of the government buildings in Washington, D.C.—including the White House, where the president lives. As luck would have it, James Madison, president at the time, was keeping the U.S. copy of the Treaty of Alliance in his office at the White House. Sadly, part of the Treaty was burned in the fire."

"Burned!" said King Evander and Sir Hector together.

The president nodded gravely and held up the photocopy of the Treaty. "You can see it here. Below this burn line, about a paragraph of the Treaty is missing. Right after the words, *'As for the field known as the Cow Park....'*"

"Then dash it, we still don't know who owns the Cow Park?" said King Evander desperately.

"Yes we do!"

It was Oliver who had said this, and he jumped up and grabbed the scroll he had brought to the Cow Park out of Sir Hector's hand. Everyone looked at him as he squeezed through the line of dark-suited men and approached the president.

"I have Patria's copy of the Treaty of Alliance right here, sir," Oliver said to the president and handed him the scroll.

"What's your name, son?" asked the president as he took the scroll.

"Oliver, sir. Oliver Stoop."

"Good to meet you, Oliver. You say this is Patria's copy of the Treaty? Where did you get it?"

"It's a long story, sir. But if you compare it to your photocopy, you'll see that it's real."

The president did as Oliver instructed, and his face broke out into a wide smile.

"Good man, Oliver Stoop. It looks like you've saved the day."

Farnsworth let out a whoop, Slobberchops yipped, and Rose cheered.

"But what does it say about the Cow Park?" said King Evander.

You could have heard the gnats nestling in the Geat warriors' beards as the president read the all-important final paragraph on the parchment Oliver had found.

"It says," declared the president finally, "that the Cow Park is to exist as an ambassadorial neutral zone."

"What does that mean?" asked Oliver.

The president turned to Oliver and placed a hand on his shoulder.

"Well, it means that while the Cow Park officially belongs to the Kingdom of Patria, the land must be used for the sole purpose of an American Embassy to Patria."

"Is that good?"

"It most certainly is, Oliver. It means that we have an end to this dispute. The war is over."

"YES!" hollered Farnsworth, and fired a whizzing biscuit into the air.

The president smiled.

The Patrian army huzzahed.

The Stoop Freedom Fighters looked thoroughly confused.

And Mr. Stoop?

He fainted.

CHAPTER SEVENTEEN
"STOOP" FOR STUPENDOUS

Sir Hector Jolly touched his knife several times to his empty glass, and the raucous conversation in the castle hall subsided into an expectant hush. With a not very gentle nudge from his daughter Lavinia, Evander Jolly IV, King of Patria, set aside the napkin upon which he had been scribbling possible titles for his epic, and rose from his seat at the head table in the full splendor of his white bow tie and tails and his royal medal glinting upon his breast.

He cast a bewildered eye upon the array of Blue Socks and Potawatomis, Geats and villagers from New Ilion. All waited for their king to say something that would capture the full depth and breadth of meaning in the occasion.

"Ah well," he began, and cleared his throat. "Here we are, aren't we? Yes, yes. Here we are. Would anyone like more cake? *Agh!*"

The king had felt the stab of Lady Lavinia's foot upon his left ankle.

"Introduce the president, Father!"

"Eh?" King Evander turned with surprise upon his counterpart seated next to him on his other side. Then he turned back to his daughter. "You mean, *he* has to talk—I don't have to?"

Titters of laughter rippled through the crowd.

"Just introduce him and *sit down* please, Father!" said Lady Lavinia with the skill of a ventriloquist as she smiled charmingly out at her guests.

"Very good," said King Evander. "Excellent. It seems, ladies and gentlemen, that I don't have to make a speech."

Huzzahs rang about the room.

"You all know how much I detest making speeches. Besides, I've just made a start on a new poem. Speaking of which, does anyone have a rhyme for "helio-copter"? *Aghghgh!*"

King Evander rubbed his left ankle and looked daggers at his daughter.

"Ladies and gentlemen," he winced, "before I sustain any further injuries, allow me to give you, once again, Patria's most distinguished friend and ally, the President of the United States—"

There was a standing ovation for the president as he, also in white bow tie and tails, rose to address the gathering.

During the applause, Oliver, seated with his friends, caught the beaming smiles of Farnsworth and Princess Rose. It had been the best of days. Everything had turned out more wonderfully than Oliver could ever have imagined.

"Thank you, ladies and gentlemen," began the president as he motioned to everyone to take their seats. "Thank you, my new friends. It is an honor to stand before you tonight as the first president of the United States to visit the Kingdom of Patria. I look forward to a long and fruitful alliance between your kingdom and our nation—though I agree with President Jefferson that it best remain a quiet one. As a confirmation of that alliance, I have today made an important decision. Too long have Patrians waited for a successor to Odysseus Murgatroyd, the great adventurer who, as the first American Ambassador to Patria, helped negotiate the original Treaty of Alliance between us. President Madison didn't agree with President Jefferson that the U.S. needed an ambassador to Patria, so the practice of naming an ambassador out here never got established. But it is high time that President Jefferson's original intention be honored. So tonight, I am proud to name the *second* American Ambassador to Patria, Mr. Reginald Stoop—"

As the hall once again rose to its feet with thunderous applause, Mr. Stoop, with a bashful wave of the hand, assumed the place of honor next to the president.

The confused reader may wonder at this point how Mr. Stoop got from lying unconscious in the Cow Park to the American ambassadorship to Patria. It all started with the carton of sour milk that Mrs. Stoop pulled out of the back corner of her refrigerator and held under her husband's nose. The remedy worked marvels, as Mr. Stoop regained consciousness instantly, batting the carton away from his face and cursing the voters who elected "that traitor of a president."

But as the Secret Service agents and Marines closed around Mr. Stoop, the president stepped forward.

"Mr. Stoop, may I have a word with you in private?"

Grudgingly, Mr. Stoop agreed to the interview, and he and the president began a lengthy stroll around the Cow Park. They walked and talked for over an hour, and when they returned, Mr. Stoop had a broad grin on his face. He whispered something in Mrs. Stoop's ear, which caused her to squeal with delight and invite the president into the mobile home for some microwave popcorn and a Mr. Phizz. With regret, the president had to decline, for he wanted to take a tour of Patria with King Evander and learn all about how Oliver had discovered the Treaty.

"Is that a real Studie?" asked the president,

admiring the car parked in the middle of the field. "Whose is it?"

"Mine, sir," exclaimed Farnsworth. "Get in. I'll give you a ride to the castle."

It was an offer the president, an old car lover, couldn't resist. So with the Marines and Secret Service creating a womb of security around the car, and with Oliver and Slobberchops riding shotgun beside him, Farnsworth drove the President of the United States, along with the new American Ambassador to Patria, to the castle. The entire way, Farnsworth lectured the president on the wonders of the Studebaker, and how he was the only kid in Patria who had one, and how everyone was (rightly) jealous of him.

Before they drove away, however, Mr. Stoop carried out the first duty assigned to him by the president.

"Pretty good battle today, eh Pete?"

"Who *are* those folks in the costumes, chief?"

Mr. Stoop caught the eye of Oliver, who seemed eager to hear how his father was going to answer this question.

"Some new friends of mine," replied Mr. Stoop as he stole a wink at his son. "They love battles as much as we do."

Oliver smiled at his father.

"I thought they was real for a minute," Pete

said, scratching his head.

"They're very good at what they do, Pete."

"Was that really the president? I mean, he kind of looked like he might be his body double. You know, for diversionary tactical purposes."

"I can neither confirm nor deny that, Pete."

"I *love* that! 'I can neither confirm nor deny that, Pete.' Hot dang! This is some wicked big re-enactment, chief. You set this all up yourself? The chopper and everything?"

"I can neither confirm nor deny that, Pete."

"Ha! Ha! Hot dang."

"I'll see you at practice on Wednesday, Pete."

"Sure, chief. Come on, boys. Where's Bill?"

Bill was already enjoying her mid-morning nap in the bed of the truck.

Oliver, Farnsworth and Rose were treated to a private lunch with King Evander, Sir Hector, and the president. Over lamb and cucumber sandwiches, they told the story of their quest for the missing Treaty, and Oliver, encouraged by Farnsworth and Rose, laid out his suspicions of Miching Malchio.

"Where is Malchio anyway?" wondered King Evander. But when he sent Sasquatch to bring Malchio and Dogsbody to him, neither of the two men could be found.

"Seems they are disappeared," reported Sasquatch.

"That's a relief," said the king. "Maybe now I can write my epic without Malchio constantly interrupting me with official business."

"I will send out my best Blue Socks to track them down," declared Sir Hector, the tips of his moustache quivering with excitement.

After lunch, Oliver, Farnsworth and Rose went for a long swim in the lake and discussed their plans for the rest of the summer. Farnsworth wanted Oliver to help him prepare for the Squire Formation Course. Rose wanted to learn how to make a biscuit that could actually be digested. As for Oliver—he just wanted to spend every minute he could in Patria.

While they were swimming, Oliver witnessed perhaps the strangest of all the strange sights he had seen that day. From the direction of the village came Sir Amory and Aunt Hazel—wearing a *summer dress.* They stopped and sat down upon a little iron bench under a solitary tree on the greensward. At one point, Aunt Hazel swung the guitar off her back and played Sir Amory a song. Although he was a good ways off, it looked to Oliver that Sir Amory, as he listened, would collapse from the sheer weight of the privilege of listening to her.

Late in the afternoon they all went in for their

baths, and at exactly seven o'clock a bell inside the castle rang, and Oliver found himself in a white bow tie and tails escorting Princess Rose into the castle hall.

After the president's introduction, Mr. Stoop made his inaugural speech as American Ambassador to Patria. First, he promised the president that even though in the morning he would resign from an absurdly well-paid position as President of the Republic of Staplers, he wouldn't hold the pay cut against the president, and that he would do his best to serve both the United States and Patria.

Second, he promised the Patrians that in summers Oliver would gladly keep the Cow Park mowed with the Lawn Beast X-Pro Groundskeeper 6000.

After the president and Mr. Stoop sat down, Sir Hector again touched his knife several times to the side of his glass. When once more the room had quieted, he instructed Sasquatch to tell the waiters to refill every glass in the room.

"I would ask that Princess Rose, Prince Farnsworth, and Master Oliver Stoop please come forward," said Sir Hector.

Shocked to hear their names called, the three friends slowly rose from their seats and, with the entire hall looking at them, took their places at the side of Sir Hector.

"Mr. President, King Evander, Chief Albert, King Ole and Queen Helga, Ambassador Stoop, and all distinguished guests—a toast is in order for this young lady, and for these two young gentlemen. Everyone, please stand."

And now the rest of the hall, including the President of the United States, stood in unison.

"These three young people have served Patria and the United States with great pluck and intelligence. A special word of thanks is due to you, Master Oliver Stoop, for the keen mind with which you puzzled out a centuries'-old mystery, and for the daring with which you brought it to light. Now all Patrians know that "Stoop" is for "stupendous.""

Oliver turned to his new, best, friends, and saw that their cheeks were burning just as much as his were.

"Working together," Sir Hector continued, "these three young people have not only held two nations back from the brink of a disastrous war, but also helped them re-forge an old alliance. With stout hearts and whizzing biscuits, they have served our peoples with great honor, and all of us must recognize how profoundly we are in their debt."

Sir Hector raised his glass.

"So please, raise a glass with me and toast our noble heroes!"

THE ADVENTURE DOESN'T HAVE TO END YET!

Go ahead and sample the following *hors d'oeuvre* (that's French for *hors d'oeuvre*)—the opening chapter of the hilarious, cavity-preventing second installment in the Kingdom of Patria series...

STOOP OF
MASTODON
MEADOW

A PATRIA Story

DANIEL McINERNY

CHAPTER ONE
SUMMER'S END

P rince Farnsworth Vesuvius awoke to find himself several feet off the ground, clutched in the hairy paw of Sasquatch, his grandfather King Evander's vaguely anthropoid butler.

"Goot mornink, Your Woyal Highness."

If you've ever had one of those dreams in which you're cornered by a gigantic Daddy Long Legs and you open your mouth to scream but no matter how hard you try no sound will come out, then you can imagine the strangled, dry-heaving sound that Farnsworth made as the fog of sleep lifted and he was faced with the sloping brow and deep-set eyes of Sasquatch some six feet above his mattress.

"Time to rise and shampoo."

And with that Sasquatch released him, and Farnsworth dropped with a muted thud onto the bed.

"It's the middle of the night, Sasquatch," groused Farnsworth into his comforter.

"Beg pardon, Your Woyal Highness. Time

exactly six hours, thirty minutes."

"That's what I said, the middle of the night."

"Breakingfast is cooking. While you take bubbles in bath, I lay out clothes for school."

Ah, school. Now Farnsworth remembered. In an attempt to put it out of his mind, he and his best friend, Oliver Stoop, the son of the American ambassador to Patria, had stayed up late watching old Western movies on Ambassador Stoop's computer, a delicacy to which Oliver had introduced him over the summer. But now the dull ache in his chest returned as Farnsworth pondered the trackless void of the next nine months.

Sliding down off the bed onto the cold floor, Farnsworth asked Sasquatch if Master Oliver was awake.

"Awake and ready."

It was Oliver himself who had said this. He was standing in Farnsworth's doorway not only awake, but bathed, combed, shined, spiffed, and otherwise as natty as bumppo. He was dressed within an inch of his life in his school blazer, matching cap, and bow tie.

"Did you even sleep last night?" Farnsworth gaped at his friend.

"Master Olywer impatient for first day at Mastodon Meadow," observed Sasquatch, with what only his closest relations would recognize as a grin.

Summer vacation was over. But Oliver, Farnsworth and Rose had enjoyed it to no end—swimming in the lake, playing Boa-Wickets on the greensward, hanging out at the Cheese Festival (the Mountain Gorgonzola, made by the monks at St. Brendan's Monastery, again won the annual Best Cheese Award).

All of this hanging out together was made easier by the fact that, soon after Mr. Stoop was made Ambassador to Patria by the President of the United States, Rose and Farnsworth's parents, Lady Lavinia and Professor Vesuvius, invited the Stoops—including Oliver's Aunt Hazel—to move into the Castle of Patria until the Stoops' new home in the Cow Park was completed. Faster than you can heat one of Mrs. Sparrow's Microwaveable Chili Corn Dogs, Mrs. Stoop had packed everyone's bags and the Stoops had settled into their new suites in the castle.

The summer, however, was not all play and no work. Farnsworth and Rose had their summer reading to do, and Oliver had years of work to make up.

Ambassador and Mrs. Stoop, you see, as a goodwill gesture toward their new friends, had decided that Oliver would advance his education that fall at the boys' school in Patria: Mastodon

Meadow. The curriculum at Mastodon Meadow is quite different than the one at Oliver's old school in Portage Head, Indiana. There is Latin, to begin with. And Greek. And seminars on the twenty-three parts of that great epic poem of the Patrian people, the *Patriad*. Oliver couldn't have been more excited about starting school at the Meadow, but he had a lot to catch up on if he wanted to join Farnsworth and the other boys his age in the Fifth Ledge that fall. Thus he spent many hours in the summerhouse by the lake being tutored by Professor Vesuvius, while Rose sat on the bench opposite reading that crown jewel of Patrian drama, *The Merry Milkmaid of the Glen*.

Farnsworth? He drifted on a raft reading *The Chronicles of Odysseus Murgatroyd, Adventurer*. Not the required summer reading, but there would be time for that (he kept telling himself) before school started again.

"How are you this morning, boys?"

Tilting the upper half of his newspaper downward, Professor Vesuvius smiled at the boys as they entered the breakfast room. Joining Professor Vesuvius at the breakfast table were King Evander, Ambassador and Mrs. Stoop, and Aunt Hazel, all eagerly tucking into the French toast, bacon, and scramblies.

"Look at our little Olly-wolly, Reginald!" cooed Mrs. Stoop, twisting in her chair to take in the full splendor of Oliver in his school uniform. Oliver was glad he hadn't eaten yet, or else he might have been sick. His mother always called him "Olly-wolly" on the first day of school.

"Don't go off before I get your picture, Oliver," said Ambassador Stoop, beaming at his son.

"I don't think there will be time for even of a rough sketch of Master Oliver before school," said King Evander.

"He means one of those colorful light pictures on his Hello-O-Phone," Professor Vesuvius corrected his father-in-law.

"Do we have to keep talking about school?" moaned Farnsworth as he shoveled French toast onto his plate from the serving tray on the sideboard. "Isn't it bad enough that we have to go? Do we have to keep rattling on about it?"

King Evander, poetically taking the rasher of bacon out of his mouth, suddenly broke into verse:

The dandelions are shriveled, their heads turned grey,
My swimming companions have all swum away—
And in the glass jar hidden under my bed
The fireflies I captured are legs up and dead.

Mrs. Stoop laid down her forkful of scrambled egg.

"I understand your emotion," said the king to her, dabbing the corner of his eye with his napkin. "It's a powerful poem. It's called "Summer's End," and was written by my great-grandfather, Fortescue Jolly."

"May I have your attention please?"

Lady Lavinia had appeared in the doorway and was smiling broadly as she trumpeted her announcement:

"I am very pleased to present to you this morning—Clarabelle Toogood, the Merry Milkmaid of the Glen!"

Lady Lavinia stepped aside and in skipped Princess Rose.

It would be bad enough, on the first day of school, to be assaulted by one's older sister literally skipping into the breakfast room. But to be assaulted by her, not only skipping, but skipping in a rose milkmaid's dress, with a rose bonnet on top of a Medusa's head of artificially-induced curls, with a *milk pail* jangling upon her arm—well, this was too much for Farnsworth. His appetite destroyed, he laid his plate down on the sideboard.

"How are you all, my goodly friends, on this fair, fine morning!" trilled Rose as she skipped about the table throwing daisies in the air. "I am the Merry Milkmaid of the Glen!"

Farnsworth slumped into his chair and asked his father if there was any more strong coffee in the pot at his elbow.

"Rose is *in character*," explained Lady Lavinia.

"When *isn't* she?" groaned Farnsworth.

"She has her first audition at school today for *The Merry Milkmaid of the Glen*." The school to which Lady Lavinia referred was none other than Madame Mimi's Well-Ordered School for Ill-Mannered Girls, run by that majestic headmistress, Madame Mimi de Pinkington de Porkington.

"Rose is going to audition for the role of—"

"Let me guess," said Farnsworth. "The Merry Milkmaid?"

Lady Lavinia twirled her napkin and swatted her son with it on the back of the head.

"I thought there was no better way to convince Madame Mimi that our Rose is the only choice for the role of the Merry Milkmaid than having her go to school in character," smiled Lady Lavinia as she took her plate to the end of the table opposite her father. "I understand, Hazel, that you have volunteered to help Madame Mimi with the costume design?"

Aunt Hazel smiled and nodded. Over the summer she had dived right into the cultural pond of Patria, taking a job as costume designer at the Blackrobe Playhouse.

Oliver filled his plate and settled into the chair next to Farnsworth.

"So Oliver!" raved Lady Lavinia. "Don't you look smart in your new school blazer! All ready for your first day at Mastodon Meadow?"

With Farnsworth in agony next to him, Oliver tried not to appear as gung ho as he felt.

"I think it'll be okay," he said.

"Now boys," Professor Vesuvius interjected, "remember that starting Thursday night you'll be staying in the dormitory at the Meadow. We're leaving for Washington, District of Columbia that morning, and so I want you all packed by Wednesday night."

Farnsworth had completely forgotten that his mother, father and grandfather were being escorted by Ambassador and Mrs. Stoop on a diplomatic trip to the capital city of the United States. He tried, but failed, to suppress a devious grin.

"How long will you be away, Father?" he asked.

"Long enough, no doubt, for you to destroy the castle, burn the village, and start a war with Mexico," Professor Vesuvius replied. "That's why I've asked Headmaster Redbreast to keep a close eye on you. Oliver, I'm sure you'll enjoy staying at the Meadow. Good food, warm beds, and an impressive library."

"It'll be good for him to be on his own," Ambassador Stoop winked at Oliver.

"And Rose, remember that you will be staying with Madame Mimi," said Lady Lavinia.

"Who's *Rose?*" inquired Farnsworth. "I don't see any Rose here. All I see is a Merry Milkmaid gorging on French toast."

Breaking character slightly, Rose grabbed the milk pail at her feet and hurled it at her brother. He ducked just in time.

"Steady, Rose," warned her mother as soon as the milk pail stopped clanging upon the floor. "Remember, you are the Merry Milkmaid. You carry sunshine in your heart wherever you go. Even though your Evil Stepmother has disowned you and sent you to live at Mr. and Mrs. Dumpfinster's Orphanage & Tobacco Store, you are never downcast. You always see the bright side of things!"

"Like the fact that mother and father will be leaving on Thursday," the Merry Milkmaid smiled brightly at her little brother. "After which I can pummel you in peace!"

Sasquatch entered the room bearing three salvers, one in each hand and one balanced neatly on top of his unusually flat head. On each salver was a large scroll tied up with a string. He presented one to Rose, one to Farnsworth, and one to Oliver.

"What's all this Sasquatch?" asked Professor Vesuvius.

Sasquatch shrugged.

"Found outside door when I put out meelk bottles. Looks like school newspaper." Sasquatch blushed. "Sorry I peek."

"School newspaper?" said Farnsworth, ripping the string off his scroll. "Delivered to the house? *Mastodon Tracks* never comes out until the end of the first week—and it's never delivered."

Farnsworth unfurled the scroll, read but for a moment, then shrieked and threw the scroll on the table. It was as if he had reacted to a skin-devouring acid in the ink.

"What is it, Farnie?" asked Lady Lavinia.

Farnsworth pointed at the scroll.

"That newspaper," he panted. "Look who published it!"

As quickly as he could Oliver ripped off the string and unfurled his scroll. His attention was gripped by the large title emblazoned across the top of it:

THE AVENGER

Underneath this ominous header was the menacing subtitle:

A NEW KIND OF SCHOOL PAPER

And underneath *that* were the publishers' names, names that had turned Farnsworth's blood to a freezer-pop in his veins:

PUBLISHED BY THE BROTHERHOOD OF
THE TUSK
&
SISTERHOOD OF THE SALON

Farnsworth's horrified reaction to these names filled Oliver with a nameless dread. And the Merry Milkmaid didn't look too merry, either. By the way she was tearing at one of her curls as she looked at her own copy of the paper, it was clear that the sunshine in her heart had given way to a hailstorm.

ABOUT THE AUTHOR

D aniel McInerny, the founder and CEO of Trojan Tub Entertainment, is a native of South Bend, Indiana (just downriver from Patria). He holds a PhD in philosophy and taught for many years at various universities in the United States. He now lives in Virginia with his wife Amy and three children, Lucy, Rita, and Francis.

Come visit us at the Kingdom of Patria!

www.kingdomofpatria.com

At the Kingdom of Patria you'll find free short stories in both text and audio, opportunities to chat with Oliver, Princess Rose, and Prince Farnsworth via their blogs, and clubs to join: either the Illustrious Order of Knights of the Blue Sock, or Madame Mimi's Well-Ordered School for Ill-Mannered Girls. Free Patria audio stories are also available at iTunes: simply search "Kingdom of Patria."

You can stay abreast of the news from Patria, as well, by joining the Trojan Tub Entertainment Facebook page, by following us on Twitter: **@kingdomofpatria**, and by joining the Trojan Tub Entertainment email list by sending your name and email address to **info@kingdomofpatria.com**.

Daniel McInerny can be contacted at **danielmcinerny@kingdomofpatria.com**.

Made in the USA
Charleston, SC
19 December 2014